THE KILLING CLUB

ALSO BY TY SCHWAMBERGER

THE KILLING CLUB

TY SCHWAMBERGER

Introduction by
John Everson

Foreword by
Paul Kane

WILDSIDE PRESS

Introduction

"Nothing in this world could ever bring them down
Yeah they're invincible, and she's just in the back-
ground
And she says
I wish that I could be like the cool kids
'Cause all the cool kids, they seem to fit in…"
—Echosmith, "Cool Kids"

It's no accident that Echosmith scored a big hit last year with a song about yearning to be a part of the in-crowd. The song is catchy enough, but it's the message that's universally attractive. Everybody's been there to some degree. And that same conceit is at the heart of Ty Schwamberger's tantalizingly disturbing tale, *The Killing Club.*

What would you do to be in the in-crowd? Smoke a cigarette and cop an attitude you don't really feel? Pretend to like things you don't? Make fun of people you do? Swear a blood pact and slice secret cuts in your arms to prove your solidarity? Set up a bucket of pig's blood over a doorway to drench the geeky girl on the head when she comes in?

What's that? None of the above? You're an outsider, you don't ever try to fit in with the in-crowd?

Bullshit.

Maybe you haven't tried to run with the Brains, or the Athletes, or the Princesses or the Criminals…to quote *The Breakfast Club.* But you've tried to fit in with someone. Maybe the Basket case. You're here reading indie horror right now, so that's my vote. Even Outsiders have social classes.

And you know what? It doesn't matter which crowd you've aligned with…there are some "cool kids" in that crowd, whatever it is, and you yearn to be numbered among them. It's human nature—we are social animals by design. It's a survival instinct. We know in our beings that as delicious as it feels sometimes to stand moody and aloof in the corner alone listening to Leonard Cohen, the only way to ensure your next meal is to get with the program.

Get with your crowd. Whichever crowd that is.

And really, finding "your" crowd, when you're a teen especially, is just as tough as getting into it. You feel the almost physical need to break away from the family, to strike out on your own... but not completely alone. What pack do you need to ally with? Do you want to join the swim club? The chess club? The LGBT club? The K Club? Who the hell knows?

The funny thing is, the desire to fit in, to be one of the cool kids...doesn't end at 18 or 21 or 30 or 50. Listen, I live in a town which may have *invented* the well-manicured cliché of the soccer mom, and you know what? All of those former sorority girls are still jockeying for position. The guys? They're working the golf course and the martini bars for a leg up. And sure, sometimes a piece of leg. One more stripe on the status dashboard.

Not me of course. I don't golf or drink vodka. Because...I'm like you. I'm an outsider. A Basket case.

Except...

I don't want to be the least of the basket cases, right? So I do my own version of the soccer mom dance. It has the soundtrack to The Cure instead of Adele...but you know what? It's all the same.

We all want to be one of the cool kids.

Do you know in fraternity and sororities, people have repeatedly submitted to serving as human garbage bags, being spit on, beat with paddles and branded with hot irons on the ass, as well as eating vomit pills, having scalding water and pepper spray poured on them, and swimming in pools of feces, semen and rotten food?

Think about that for a while, before you say, "nah, nobody would ever do *that* to fit in."

Oh yeah? For that endorphin thrill of belonging, anything is fair game.

Deny it all you want...but deep down, we all want to be with the cool kids. Desperately. Some people will literally eat shit to do it. Some, would no doubt, be prepared to kill.

Would you?

—John Everson

Foreword

Reading this story, by award-winning author and editor Ty Schwamberger, is little like being parachuted in behind enemy lines, then coming under heavy fire and finally having to be rescued by a Black Ops team, dragged through a no man's land and hoping you make it out alive.

In short, you're left reeling and feel a bit like you've been in a war.

Ostensibly the story of two teenage girls—on the one side, Sherry, who apparently has the perfect family life, and on the other side down on her luck Kristen who accidentally finds herself getting sucked into a world she has no experience of, and little resistance to—this story has much wider implications. It's about conformity and control, about peer pressure and trying to fit in, whatever the cost. It's about modern life and how we find our place in society, or how we don't.

And it's about killing, *lots* of killing.

Schwamberger is very good at presenting a scene that looks almost normal, then tweaking it here and there—giving us little details that just feel at odds with the rest of what's being described—so that by the time you realize you might be in David Lynch territory, it's already way too late and the horrors have begun. His ability to build tension and unease is top notch, and some of these chapters are a master class in unbearable suspense. If you thought *The Strangers* was good at making you scared of knocking on the other side of a closed door, then you haven't seen anything yet.

His characters feel real, with real lives and real concerns—taking you inside their heads to get their point of view on things. And that's important too, when you want your reader to care about what happens to them next. The kind of bitchiness that goes on at school between girls is particularly well rendered, in fact. The sort that might drive someone to do stupid things; things they will ultimately regret.

Then there are those shock moments that good horror fiction—hell, good horror in general—rely on. Blood-soaked encounters, descents into underground terror and surprise reveals all await the intrepid explorer here—if they have enough balls to turn the pages. But be warned, once you start, you're not going to stop until the entire adrenalin-fuelled journey is over—I read it in one, nail biting sitting and I suspect you'll probably be compelled to do the same. There's a reason one family is named the Laymons, a nod—surely—to one of the finest horror masters America has ever produced.

A suburban nightmare, this tale is made all the more disturbing by the fact that it could happen; all it would take would be the right circumstances and a bit of a push.

So, are you ready to be dropped in? Are you sure?

Then go ahead and turn the next page, and get ready to start living on your nerves…

—Paul Kane
Derbyshire, UK
January 2016

Chapter 1

"So how was your day, sweetie?" her mother asked, sticking a fork-full of lima beans into her mouth. She smiled as she chewed, looking at her daughter.

Sherry pushed around some of the beans on her own plate and said, "Eh, okay I guess. I mean, being a freshman is kinda the pits."

"Why's that?" her father asked through a mouthful of grilled chicken.

"I don't know," Sherry replied, turning her head from her mother to her father. "I mean, I guess it's okay, ya know. But, some of the upper-classmen are kinda bunch of jerks. Especially, the girls. There's this one girl, Katie, she has to be the worst of them."

"Why's that?" her mother asked.

"Cause, she thinks her sh…err…stuff don't stink. One of those-kinda-girls."

"Yeah, I remember a few of those myself," her father said, smiling at Sherry's mother.

"Hey."

"Now, now, dear. I don't mean *you*, of course," her father said, quickly regaining control of the quip. "What I meant was that I understand where Sherry is coming from. If you remember correctly, Julie, there were a couple girls in our class that were jerks, too."

Sherry's mother, seemingly remembering back some twenty-five years then said, "Yeah, I guess you're right, Stanley. I do remember a few choice girls that didn't like the fact that you and I were dating back in high school. In fact, do you remember Sally Dunewright? Now she was a real piece of work. She didn't like you with me from the beginning. If I remember correctly, she wanted you to take her to Prom instead of me. She spread some rumors around school that weren't very nice and hurt my reputation for a while. Well, that is, until I got her back."

"Yeah, I do believe I remember that quite well," Sherry's father replied, then started laughing. Her mother joined in a moment later. The next thing Sherry knew; both her parents were really busting a gut. If they had had food in their mouths, it would have been spewing all over the table.

Sherry looked at her little brother, Frankie, and shrugged her shoulders. Frankie stared back at her with a blank look in his eyes. He then went back to scooping a fork-full of beans off his plate, shoving them into his gaping mouth.

Sherry still didn't understand how the kid could enjoy eating such a putrid vegetable as lima beans. It was his favorite vegetable, actually the only kind he would eat without someone having to stuff some in his mouth and hold his nose till he swallowed. Sherry really didn't understand her mother's 'health food' kick that she was trying on them. None of them were unhealthy per say, yet they all had to equally suffer the consequences of her new obsession. She guessed she could understand her mother wanting her father to eat better, as he was a tad overweight (at least that is what she overheard her parents talking about one night when she was supposed to be asleep, but instead was at the top of the stairs, listening to her father tell about his recent check-up at the doctor's office) but was still very handsome and relatively fit for a man of his age.

What am I talking about, Sherry thought. *It's not like he's ancient or anything. What is he now, forty-three, forty-four, something like that? Heck, he's a lot younger than a lot of my friends' parents are.* Sherry also knew her father's love of ice cream pies and tortilla chips, which he ate by the box and bag full. Those tasty and lovable items were a thing of the past inside the Laymon residence. They were now replaced by health foods, such as: chicken (no more red meat—*God, I miss cheeseburgers on the grill*), plenty of vegetables (mostly lima beans—*damn you, Frankie*), juice (no more soda of any kind—*what Mom doesn't know I drink at school won't hurt her*), and if her mother was feeling real generous one night, fish (salmon—*gross*).

Sherry looked away from Frankie, who was busy shoving tasteless grilled chicken and lima beans into his mouth, and turned her head from her mother to her father. They were both still laughing, though not as hard as before. After a few glances back and forth they finally quieted down.

Sherry let out a long breath, reaching over her plate and grabbing her glass-full of apple juice (*now this* is *the pits, folks*). She took a small sip of the tart yellow-brown liquid and quickly set it back down onto the table. She cleared her throat and looked at her mother, who was still smiling; evidently still remembering whatever she had done that was so funny so many years ago.

"What?" her mother finally asked Sherry, who was staring at her slack-jawed.

"So…you gonna tell us what happened or what?"

"Nah."

"*Nah?* You and Dad are busting a gut over here and you can't even tell us what's so funny about the prank you pulled on this girl? Hey. Who knows, maybe it'll be good enough for me to use to get back at that bi…err…Katie for treating me how she does."

"Oh sweetie…" her mother began. Then, "It doesn't do any good to try and get back at someone just because you don't like them or they did something not-so-nice, you know? You have to 'kill 'em with kindness.' How many times have I told you and your brother that?"

Sherry shrugged her shoulders then said, "I don't know. Maybe a billion and one?" and started laughing. Frankie, not paying her or anyone else much attention before, started laughing as well. Sherry felt good; even though Frankie was five years younger than her, and most of the time a royal pain in the you-know-where, he was finally on her side. She didn't know if he truly understood the joke or not. He was ten and should know a good joke (that wasn't about farts or someone's tiny willy) when he heard one, but Sherry couldn't be so sure. But, she also knew it wasn't the time to ask him. Maybe later but not right now. Oh, no. Right now felt too good for the two of them to be laughing, together. Just her and her brother. Really busting a gut of their own. It felt wonderful.

Finally, after the laughing started to die down, she looked at her mother. Her face was red. Big pink veins were sticking out of her forehead. She was pissed and Sherry knew it. She had crossed the line by insulting her mother. She was done-for. Sherry quickly looked at her father, her protector, for some support. He just shrugged his shoulders as if saying, "I'm sorry sweetie, your mother rules the roost around here and I couldn't speak my mind even if I wanted to." Sherry gave her father a quick nod as if saying, "I get ya. No hard feelings" and looked back to her mother and said, "Hey. I'm sorry, Mom. Really. I didn't mean to backtalk. Honest. I thought we were all having a good time here, ya know? I didn't mean to insult you or whatever. Heck, you and Dad were just laughing at some girl you messed with back when you two were in high school so I thought it was okay to add a joke of my own. Really. I'm sorry. Okay?"

As Sherry waited for the veins on her mother's forehead to explode and shower her with blood, she thought about how much her mother had changed, especially during the last month.

Before her father had gotten back from the doctors and told her about his latest check-up, she had been what they call a 'mother of the year candidate.' But since then, her mother had changed and it didn't all have to do with changing the diet of everyone in the house. She seemed less even-tempered than before, more stressed out, less loving, more overbearing, yelling at her and her brother more (*Heck, now that I think about it, I can only remember one time in my life prior to a month ago when she yelled at me and that was when I was five and left my bike in the driveway and Dad backed over it in the morning when he was pulling out of the garage on his way to work. He didn't get angry, of course, by God, he did name me for petesakes after his favorite performer, Frankie Valli—me and my brother—so he didn't care much, but Mom sure did. I remember her screaming about how I was a worthless little kid and never listened and blah, blah, blah...the whole nine yards, ya know. But that had been about it for more than ten years. Shoot. Now all of a sudden that Dad might be a little overweight she's going off the handle about stupid stuff. Geez)* and she was gone from the house more often than not. Before about a month ago, she had been the typical 'soccer Mom' toting Sherry and her brother to this place and that for school functions and from their friends' houses. But now—all the good stuff that had once been Sherry's mother was gone. Mostly. Sherry had thought when they sat down for supper that her mother had seemed in a pretty good mood by asking how her and Frankie's days went at school, remembering the good ol' days, joking, laughing, all that. Sherry had started to believe that tonight would be the first night of the rest of their happy lives. Her mother would return to being the soccer Mom/loving wife she had been for the first fifteen and a half years of her life.

But, one wrong word had turned everything ugly.

Sherry looked from her mother to Frankie—now shoveling beans and pieces of chicken into his mouth as quickly as possible—then back to her mother.

Just in time to see her mother's hand flying toward her face.

SMACK!

"Hey!" Sherry shouted, grabbing the right side of her face. "What the fuck did I do to you? You bitch."

Sherry couldn't believe those words actually came out of her mouth but they had. She looked at her brother. Frankie threw his fork on his plate and started crying into his hands. She loved her brother very much, even if he was a pain in the butt sometimes, and hated to see him hurting like he was right now. She would have to console him later, tell him everything was going to be okay, even though she had no idea right now if it ever would be again.

Her still-loving father put a hand on her shoulder. Even though she knew it wasn't his fault, hoped it wasn't his fault, she jerked away from him and stood up. The back of her legs hit the seat of the chair, sending it flying behind her. It slammed against the wall.

Her brother started screaming, "Please…please…just stop it… all of you just stop it" over and over again.

Sherry didn't bother looking at her father again as she ran from the table. Her mother reached, trying to grab her arm, but she was too fast. Her mother's long nails scratched her skin as Sherry twisted away from her. She bolted from the dining room, through the living room and made a quick turn to the left, ready to pound up the stairs.

That's when it happened.

A high-pitched sound broke through the screams of her mother, the cries coming from her little brother, the shouting from her father at her mother, everything.

Holding onto her wrecked left arm and feeling something warm running in between her fingers, Sherry twisted around to where the sound was coming from.

The familiar high-pitched sound radiated through the tense air inside the house again.

The doorbell.

Sherry almost hoped that one of their next door neighbors had heard the commotion and called the cops but didn't think it was possible. *Besides*, Sherry thought, *except when I screamed at Mom there wasn't much else going on that the Roger's or Rose's could have heard. I mean, I was the first one to start screaming.* As those thoughts ran through Sherry's mind, she could still hear the commotion coming from the dining room—her father yelling, her mother yelling, her brother crying—all of it. *Of course*, Sherry continued thinking, *now everyone's in an uproar. Shoot. I wouldn't be surprised if the whole neighborhood couldn't hear us now. We probably always seemed like the picture-perfect family up until the last month or so and now look at us.*

The doorbell sounded once more.

Shit.

Sherry didn't know what to do. On one hand: she really should see who was at the door (during her mother's good-days she had taught her that if you're home, even if it is a Jehovah Witness or someone else that drives people nuts peddling their bullshit from door to door that it wasn't polite to keep people waiting past the second ring). On the other: all she really wanted was to run upstairs to her room, lock the door, and not come out until morning when it was time to go to school.

Hell with that bull. I'm taking a sick day tomorrow. I'm tired of dealing with the upper-classmen girls at school, and now Mom is totally off her rocker. This should qualify me for a day home from school. Heck. Maybe I can get Dad to call in for me.

If any of us survive tonight, especially with the way Mom is acting. 'Total nut-job of the year,' is more like it, Sherry thought, chuckling inside.

Sherry swiveled around on the third step from the bottom of the stairs and trotted back down.

The heck with it. I hope it's the cops. Then they can hall Mom to jail for the night and sleep the bitchiness off.

Yeah. Sherry liked the sound of that.

The Bitch Tank.

HA HA.

The doorbell rang a third time.

Third time's a charm, as they say. Well, maybe not.

Sherry came up to the door, reached out and grabbed the doorknob. She could still hear the commotion in the dining room, but it seemed to be quieter now.

Mom probably thinks it is the cops and is trying to talk Dad into letting her stay the night and not take her to the bitch tank, instead.

Sherry smiled, twisted the knob and pulled.

The door swung open.

A girl, not much older the Sherry stood on the stoop.

Covered in bright red blood.

Sherry had a sudden rush of what tasted like pennies in the back of her throat.

Blood.

Covering the girl from the top of her head down to her bare toes. She wasn't wearing a stitch of clothes.

Sherry and the blood-covered girl locked eyes.

But, it was just for a moment.

Because that was all it took for the girl to fall against Sherry, knocking her to the floor.

Sherry tried to scream as her rump hit the floor, followed by her back, and her head bounced off the hardwood flooring. She could still hear the commotion coming from the dining room and realized that even if she did manage to choke out a scream that no one would be able to hear it.

Sherry blacked out with the blood-covered girl still lying on top of her.

Chapter 2

Sherry woke up to darkness all around, her head still pounding from the collision with the floor. She drew her right hand from under the top sheet that was covering her and fingered the back of her skull. She winced. She could tell a big fat goose egg had formed from her fall to the floor. She flung the sheet off her body. With the moonlight filtering through her bedroom window, she saw how the breeze was coming into her room grabbing hold of the sheet; making the thin fabric drift through the air for a second or two before it landed in a rumpled pile at her knees. With the sheet off her body, she could feel cool air blowing into her room. Sherry then threw her legs off the bed and started to stand up. A dizzy spell hit her and she quickly fell back down to her pillow.

Whoa, that was close, she said. *That's all I need right now is to get dizzy, pass out, and do a* face-plant *into the floor. Better stay right where I'm at till I can get Mom or Dad to help me walk.*

The thought of her mother and father, and even her pesky brother, Frankie, made a tidal wave of blood-covered memories rush back to her.

Oh my God! What happened to the girl at the door?

Sherry knew she had to find out what happened to the girl: was she dead on arrival, as they liked to say on the hospital shows on television, or after her parents (she figured it was her mother and father, anyway) tended to her, making sure that she would live and carried her up to her room where she was lying in her own bed now, helped the poor girl, calling the police and 911 to come to the rescue. Sherry didn't know, but she knew she had to find out.

She really did look about my age. I wonder if I know the girl... Does she go to Oakwood High like me? If so, have I seen her around before? If I have, why didn't I recognize her after I opened the door?

Those were some of the thoughts running through Sherry's head. But then she remembered the blood.

Oh, God. There was so much blood.

Guess that makes sense, Sherry continued to think through the ordeal. *Even if I do know the girl, it might be pretty hard to recognize someone, even after seeing them on a daily basis, with them all covered in blood like that.*

All that blood.

There had been tons of it—from head to toe.

Sherry remembered how naked the girl had been. The girl, whatever her name, hadn't been wearing a thing. She was naked right down to her socks. And even though Sherry was into boys, especially Warren, the Freshman class president, she was still able to take in the beauty of the female form without feeling like if she did look at a naked girl in the showers after volleyball practice or gym class, that it wouldn't make her into a poon-lovin' hound or anything remotely close to one. She was confident enough in her own sexuality (not that Sherry knew much about the actual 'act' of sex since she was still technically a virgin—though she had let Jimmy 'Fingers' Clauson feel her up in eighth grade—but she knew that was only second base and still a long way off from rounding third and 'sliding' into home, as some of the kids still called it) that looking at a naked girl from time to time (and also knowing that there were probably friends of hers in the same gym class or when one of them would spend the night and they would change into their pajamas before climbing into bed) didn't make her into a lesbian. In fact, the thought never had crossed her mind that she might be. She knew she had a healthy non-sexual appetite that wouldn't mold her into something that she wasn't just because she looked (and girls looked at her) at a girl from time to time. Though, now that Sherry thought about it, maybe she had been looking a little too much lately at the girls in the shower after practice or gym class. She never thought much about the act until right now, but now that she was pondering it, it did scare her a tad.

Maybe I am a lesbian, but still in the closet?

Oh my God.

What if Mom and Dad find out that I like girls? They'll never trust me having Stacey or Meghan over her ever again.

Nah. There's no way I am a lesbian or a poon-hound. I'm a normal, everyday teen girl that just so happens to admire the female form from time to time.

That was Sherry's story, and she was sticking to it.

Sherry knew she had to find out what happened to the girl. She could always call for Mom and Dad to come into the room (and even Frankie, if need be), but if they were still waiting on the paramedics to arrive (Sherry still had no idea how long she had been unconscious at this point and even with glancing at the red numbers on her alarm clock it still didn't help since she had no recollection as to what time it had been when she stormed out of the dining room, was about to go running up the stairs to her room, when the doorbell rang and she turned around and opened it—to a naked, bloody girl standing on the stoop and who then fell on top of her and knocked her to the floor where she banged her head), she didn't want to be the one to call one of them away when they were helping someone more injured than herself. So, instead of calling out for her parents or Frankie to come to her aid, Sherry took a deep breath, tightened her stomach muscles, and forced herself into a sitting position on the edge of the bed.

So far, so good.

She hadn't felt it when she had been standing up the first time, but now she could really feel the full force of the cold autumn air that was coming through her open window and blowing against her bare arms. She wished that her parents had taken off the short-sleeved shirt and jeans that she had worn to school and replaced them with a nice, clean pair of long-armed and legged pajamas. Then, she wouldn't be cold like she was now. Even with the faint light coming into her room from the moon, she could see the goose-flesh popping up all over her skin. She crossed her arms over her chest, could feel her hard nipples trying to poke through the red, cotton shirt, took another deep breath and stood up. She swayed a few times but was able to keep her balance this time. She slowly started walking to the right side of the room where her dresser was located.

I'll get something warmer on and slowly go downstairs and

see if I can help out in any way. I mean, the girl has to still be here. Mom and Dad are probably trying to keep her alive until the paramedics get here and can take over. Maybe they are even busy cleaning off all the blood that was on the girl. Yeah. That would make sense. Dad probably carried me up to my room and tucked me in (being a Daddy's girl and all), *while Mom attended to the girl; helping her to the couch and telling her everything was going to be alright as she ran to the phone to call 911, returning to a small bowl and washcloth to help clean the blood off her body.*

Sherry reached her dresser, pulled out the second to bottom drawer, and pulled out her favorite long-sleeved and legged pajamas—Winnie the Pooh and Tigger, too. Sherry smiled at the thought, as she dropped the pajamas on the floor, stripped off her crusty shirt and jeans (she left her bra and panties on, as they didn't seem to be caked with dried blood. Sherry wondered why her father hadn't changed her before putting her in bed and covering her up with a clean sheet, except that maybe he had been too shy to do such a thing to his daughter or that he was just in too much of a hurry to get her to safety and help out the more injured girl was downstairs with her mother), tossed them into the corner of the room, then bent down and grabbed the pajama bottoms. She stepped into one leg at a time and pulled the top of the pants up until they fit snug around her trim waist. She was about to bend down to pick up the pajama shirt, but decided to take off her bra, anyway. She never slept with one on—it always seemed to be crushing her chest—so she reached behind her, undid the fastener, and slid the flimsy, white garment off her shoulders and down her thin arms. She threw the bra on top of the other dirty clothes in the corner of the room. Then she bent down, again, grabbed her pajama shirt, sporting Pooh Bears' happy face on the upper left corner, and slid it up her arms, over her head and pulled it till the bottom of the shirt reached the top of her pants.

Now she felt ready. For what, she still had no idea. But she felt that if everyone else in the house was still helping the poor girl, then she should too.

Just because I knocked my noodle on the floor and passed out for awhile doesn't mean I'm an invalid or something. I can always sit there and hold a cool, damp rag over the girl's head or some-thing...maybe I can even help Mom clean the girl up. Yeah, that would be nice to do. I would rub a nice, warm washcloth over the girl's skin, getting her all squeaky clean and everything. I could rub the tops of her shoulders and to her chest and rub her...

Sherry stopped herself from thinking anything else related to touching the breasts of the girl downstairs. She then quickly slammed the dresser drawer shut and started walking to her bed-room door. As she walked across the cold, wooden floor (*God, I should have gotten Mom to buy me a rug or something...I'm freez-ing my toes off here*) she still felt a little dizzy, but it wasn't as bad as before.

Finally, she reached her bedroom door. She stood there, staring blankly at the door, still a little dizzy and half scared. The dizziness she could deal with. Not knowing what became of the injured girl made her bowels tighten. As Sherry grabbed the knob, she really hoped the girl was okay and that Mom and Dad were taking great care of her until the paramedics arrived and were able to do the fabulous job she had always seen them do on the television. Yes, Sherry knew the difference between real-life and a T.V. show, but since she had never had any first-hand experience with paramed-ics, she always figured that the actors and actresses on some of her favorite prime-time shows had to have had some sort of training before playing a role on *ER* or *House* with their real-life counter-parts and therefore the stories on T.V. were probably closer than one might think. Sherry didn't know for sure but guessed that this was probably correct.

She twisted the knob and pulled.

As the door swung slowly toward her, she could feel the door trying to pull out of her grasp and heard a vacuum-type sound. She glanced behind her and noticed that the once fluttering cur-tains were now pressed tightly against the screen inside the win-dow. She shivered and felt the gooseflesh return to her skin. Even with the long-sleeved and legged pajamas she was still chilly. She hoped that Mom had made some hot coca for the injured girl and would have enough to offer her some once she got downstairs.

I'll give that to Mom. She might be acting crazy for the past month or so, but she always seems to find a tender place in her heart for making her and Dad, Frankie and I are still taken care of.

Sherry made a mental note to sit down with her mother and have a heart-to-heart once tonight's events were behind them. They had always been close before (well, not as close as her and her father were, of and Sherry knew that she wanted it back.

That's exactly what I'll tell Mom, too, Sherry said to herself as she exited her room and walked across the hall and went inside the bathroom. She closed the door behind her, walked to the toilet, pulled down her pajama pants and panties and sat down. The cold toilet seat shocked her buttocks for a second but then felt okay. As she sat all the way down, starting to urinate, she thought more about her mother and her relationship and how it had been on the rocks for the past several weeks. She vowed to herself that she would fix it after all of them (yes, even Frankie) helped the girl until the paramedics arrived and took her to a hospital for further care. Yes, she would patch things up with her mother and maybe even try to be a little nicer to her sometimes-bratty brother (she didn't need to do anything special for her father since she was daddy's girl and all) and all of them could return to how things were before things started to go down the crapper a month ago.

After urinating, Sherry stood up, pulled her pants and panties up to her waist, flushed the toilet, washed and dried her hands, then walked to the bathroom door. Since her bladder was now empty she felt even better now than she had before. Yes, she was still a bit dizzy, but she could deal with it.

She reached down and grabbed the doorknob.

I'll ask Mom to get me a few aspirin and after I take them, I'll probably feel good as new.

She twisted the knob. It turned all the way to the left.

She pulled.

The door didn't swing back toward her.

It seemed stuck somehow.

Twisting the knob back and forth a few times, Sherry tried opening the door, again.

Nothing.

What the... The damn thing must be locked or something.

Sherry twisted the knob back and forth a few more times, while trying to pull the door open.

It was no use.

Even though she hadn't wanted to call for her mother or father, taking them away from someone that was clearly in more trouble for just being locked in a bathroom and all but she didn't have much choice. She wanted to see how the girl was doing and help her parents, if need be.

She called out for her mother and father. She even called out Frankie's name.

Nothing.

"Hey guys!" Sherry screamed. "I need some help. Somebody. Anybody. Heeelllooo…is anybody out therrre? I'm locked inside the upstairs bathroom and can't get the door open. I think it might be locked or something."

No reply came from her mother, father, or her little brother.

"Come on guys…this isn't funny anymore. I really need some help. Heeellloooooo?"

That's when someone knocked on the opposite side of the door and started laughing.

Chapter 3

"You sure you have everything, sweetie?"

"For the hundredth time, yes, Mom."

"Did you pack your toothbrush? Remember what Doctor Marco said, 'Kristen, you really need to start brushing after every meal. You're getting a bunch of gunk caught in between those chompers of yours.' Remember?"

"Again. Yes, Mom…I remember what Doctor Marco told me. Geez."

"Don't 'geez' me, young lady. Who do you think will have to pay for you to get dentures if all your teeth rot and fall out? Huh? Yeah, me, that's who. So, if Doctor Marco tells you that you need to start brushing your teeth after every meal or else they'll start to rot beyond, well, by-golly, you're gonna brush those puppies even after eating one Jelly Belly."

Kristen didn't reply. Instead, she turned her head away from her mother and stared out at passing lawns, trees, and houses from the passenger side window. Most of the homes were dark. Kristen figured that since it was a Friday night, the majority of the occupants were out having dinner or catching a movie down at Slippery Sliders, the town's local pizza joint/movie theatre.

Actually, it wasn't much of a movie theatre at all, but Kristen had to admit that each time she had gone there with her folks and younger brother; they had always had a good ol' time. The idea behind the restaurant/movie place was pretty simple: you would walk up to the counter, order a pie, and buy a ticket to which movie you would want to see. There were a total of six rooms to the large building: the lobby, where you would place your pizza and movie ticket order, and five somewhat smaller rooms. After ordering a pie and your tickets, the pimple-faced dweeb behind the counter would hand you a ticket and inform you which of the five 'theatres' you would be dining in for the night. You would then waltz on to whatever specific room the movie you wanted to see was playing in, go inside, and wait for your pie to be delivered. You had to time things just right if you wanted the combo—dinner and a movie—if you got there too late and the movie was about to start, you were pretty much shit out of luck for being able to eat during the movie. Sure, you could buy everyday-movie-type-snacks and drinks and not have pizza, but what was the point of going to the Slippery Sliders (Kristen never understood why they had the word 'sliders' in the name—the place didn't serve tiny burgers, only pizza) if you weren't going to order a pie and watch a movie. If you didn't want to have the combo, you might as well drive to the next town over, and buy your snacks, drinks, and tickets at a real theatre and see whatever—horror, romance, or comedy—flick you wanted to see. Kristen's family never had seen much point in going to an ordinary theatre, so when Slippery Sliders opened up four years ago in the same town they lived in, and especially after experiencing the fun of having someone deliver your pizza a half hour before the movie started and about the time you finished with dinner the show started, they hadn't driven to the old theatre in Brainbridge. They always had a rip roaring good ol' time at Slippery Sliders. Yup, they sure did.

God, how she loved her family. She even loved her Mom, who could be a real pain the butt sometimes when she went on and on about stupid stuff. Well, Kristen thought it was stupid, anyway. Hell, she was seventeen now and figured that most people her age still didn't get hassled by their parents about making sure to pack a toothbrush and brush-brush-brush their teeth after every meal. Then again, Kristen did understand that it would be her parents' dime if her teeth did rot out of her skull and she had to get all fake ones, especially after the bad news coming from her last check-up with Doctor Marco, so she guessed her mother did have a right to bitch at her. But that didn't mean she should like it. Kristen heard sounds still coming from her mother's mouth but wasn't really paying attention. She was still watching the houses pass them by, wondering what the families in the still-lighted houses were doing right now if they weren't at the town's favorite eatery getting all fat on greasy (really it was remarkably delicious) pizza and watching a new flick on one of the five fifteen-foot screens that Slipper's Sliders had in each enclosed room. She guessed she would find out soon enough. She was excited but filled with dread all at the same time.

Kristen's mother made a left and started the climb up the steep hillside on which Kia's parents' house sat. Sputtering and choking its way up the smoothly paved driveway, the old family station wagon finally reached the crest. The driveway spread out in each direction from there. A fountain sat in the middle of the vast circular driveway. It had a naked, chubby cherub standing on top of a tall platform in its middle. One of the cherub's hands held a bow and arrow. The other was holding its tiny stone penis. A steady stream of water shot out its end. The entire fountain was illuminated by dark blue and green lights.

Steering the car around the fountain, with its naked, chubby, pissing baby in its center, Kristen's mother pulled up behind a shiny red Porsche and turned back the ignition key. The car sputtered a few more times, then died. Kristen was glad the junkyard-on-wheels didn't backfire as it had while her mother was dropping her off on the first day at her new school. That was the first time she encountered the four most popular senior girls at Oakwood's private all-girls' school—Smithshire Academy.

Kristen still didn't fully understand how a town of no more than thirty-thousand residents could support the needed enrollment of two high schools but figured that it was because the town was pretty much fifty-fifty with those who had money and could afford to send their daughters to the expensive private school and those who were unfortunate to not have much money at all and therefore had to send their daughters and sons to the town's public high school—Oakwood High. Kristen's family was one of the unfortunate ones—her mother had worked as a cashier at the local Piggly Wiggly for the past ten years and her father was a mechanic down at the Mobile gas station down on the corner of Walnut and 55th Street. So, no, Kristen's family didn't have a lot of money. The fact of the matter was, Kristen's family couldn't even come close to affording one semester at the prestigious private, all-girls' school, let alone the next year and a half of her high school education. The only way she was even attending the private school was that Kristen had been the lucky recipient of a scholarship the end of her sophomore year at Oakwood High with the rest of the poor kids. The gist of the scholarship was whoever not only had the best grades at the end of their sophomore year at Oakwood High but also showed the most potential (and could score high enough on an IQ test, pass a physical, and answer correctly while being lambasted with questions from the Board of Directors at Smithshire Academy) would be the lucky winner of the scholarship and therefore be able to attend the private school free of charge (as long as their grades remained at or above a 4.0) for the rest of their high school career.

So, after her mother's piece-of-shit-on-wheels pulled up to the all marble, pillared entrance on her first day of school on her junior year, it had backfired right after Kristen had said her goodbyes to her mother and was about to step out of the car and try to keep her chin held high (like all the other rich bitches that went to the school that thought their shit smelled like peaches and cream and red roses on steroids). That's when her mother's car let out a gigantic…*BOOM!* And all the girls who were still being dropped off by their parents in their fancy BMWs and Mercedes and Porches and the like and the ones who were just standing around and shooting the proverbial shit, hit the deck like they were in Vietnam and a platoon of chinks were throwing grenades in their direction.

After the car pulled away and the smoke coming from her mother's rusted out tailpipe blew away in the breeze, that's when four of the most beautiful but biggest bitches on two-legs came striding up to her and started screaming at her. "What the fuck is a white piece of trailer trash like you doing here?" and "Your Mom's hooptie is a nice looking automobile. Where can my Dad buy one for me?" Then one of the four blonde bitches spit in Kristen's face and laughed. The other three didn't take their turns spitting in her face but must have thought it was a real gut-buster because they all laughed so hard that tears come out of their eyes then doubled-over, clutching their stomachs, evidently from how much physical pain they were in, at Kristen's expense. Fortunately, Kristen hadn't been hurt physically that first day at her new school, but she was emotionally crushed, and sometimes that was even worse than being punched in the gut or kicked in the nuts—if you happened to be a guy, that is.

So, yes, Kristen was very happy that her mother's shitty car didn't backfire this time. It was a huge relief.

The only problem now was: why had Kia invited her to her parents' house tonight and what sort of emotional trauma was she going to have to go through while being ten miles away (Kristen's parents lived on a farm on the outskirts of town but were still technically residents of the Oakwood school system) away from her own parents' house with no way to get back home if things got too bad.

Her mother was still saying or asking her something, but Kristen just shrugged her shoulders, said, "Yeah, okay," over and over again, leaned over and kissed her mother goodbye and stepped out of the car. Her mother waved through the passenger side window, then started the car and began to pull away. Part of Kristen wanted to run after her mother's car, screaming, "Wait, no. I don't wanna spend the night, after all. How about all of us go down to Slippery Sliders and get a pizza pie and catch a comedy (God, she could really use a nice funny movie to forget how badly nervous she felt right now about being at Kia's house and having to spend the night with three other of The K-Club girls) or something." But she didn't. Nope. Instead, Kristen watched her mother's car pull away until it vanished over the top of the hill they had driven up together just a few minutes before.

Kristen knew she was on her own.

God, she wanted to be popular like The K-Club girls were at Smithshire Academy—popular but still nice to all the other girls that weren't fortunate enough to be part of the most elite non-club club in school.

Maybe I can change them if I just explain how they make other people feel, Kristen thought as she spun around and started walking up the marble steps at the front of the gigantic house that loomed high overhead.

She reached the stoop and pressed the lighted doorbell. She

could hear a chorus of dings and bells fill the inside of the house.

As she waited for Kia or another one of The K-Club girls to answer the door, she said to herself, *I must be as crazy as Kia, Kelly, Kara and Kristina are, if I'm standing here right now, about to go inside the lion's den and face the fire. Besides, what the hell do they want with a girl like me? I mean, I guess I'm not ugly by any stretch of the imagination, but I'm certainly no Kia or Kelly… They're fabulous…Kara and Kristina are okay, I guess. But, really. What in the world do they want with someone normal, like me? Shit. What in the world am I getting myself into? Geez, Kristen! You must be a whack job yourself if you think that Kia invited you over here tonight to become friends. Damn. I'm screwed.*

Suddenly the front door swung open, snapping Kristen out of her worry-filled thoughts.

Kia.

The perfect-everything girl smiled then said, "Hey there, *Kristen*, nice of you to make it tonight. Come on in, sweets."

"Hey." Kristen mumbled, stepping past Kia into the home's vast front foyer.

Kia shut the door and came up within an inch or two of Kristen's face. Kristen could feel the hot exhale coming from Kia's nose. They were that close. So close that if Kia really wanted to, she could lunge forward and bite off Kristen's nose even before Kristen knew what happened. Then the joke would be on Kristen because she was not only dumb enough for coming to Kia's house to spend the night and be their friend but now because she was gushing blood out of her partial chewed off nose all over the beautiful marble floor she was afraid to even be standing on. She made a mental note to take off her shoes as soon as Kia was done doing whatever she was about ready to do.

God…I hope she doesn't bite…

Kia's slender face suddenly bolted forward.

Oh My God…She's gonna head butt me!

Then Kia's soft, pouty lips met Kristen's.

They felt even more wonderful than when Kristen had kissed Dean Harrison for the first time in fifth grade on top of the jungle gym during recess.

Kia's mouth stayed on top of Kristen's. It was the most beautiful, soft kiss that Kristen had ever had in her entire life (not that she was all that experienced with boys—though, she had let Tommy Erb feel her up while they were making out one time at the Slippery Slider while watching Scream 175 or whatever the fuck part they were on at the time).

Then just as quickly as Kia had leaned in to steal the kiss from Kristen, she pulled away. She smacked her delicate, wet lips together and said, "Well, come on. What are you waiting for *Kristen*? Huh? All The K's are waiting for us downstairs. *We* better get a move on."

As she followed Kia from the foyer through the dining room, two bonus rooms, a den, the kitchen, and through a door and down a flight of steps to the basement where the rest of The K-Club girls were waiting on them, Kristen said to herself, *Holy shit. I can't believe I missed it before. 'K.' The K-Club. All their fucking names start with the letter 'K.' Holy smokestacks…and so does mine.*

As Kristen followed Kia down the well-lit flight of stairs and heard the other girls talking and laughing and music playing in the background, she wondered if getting invited to Kia's house because her name started with the letter 'K' was a good or bad thing.

She guessed she would find out soon enough.

The three other girls already downstairs cheered when Kristen and Kia came into the room.

Kristen didn't know if she felt like smiling or shitting her pants.

She was glad her Mom was so anal and reminded her about a hundred times "to bring two extra pairs of panties, because you never know when you might have an accident."

Kristen smiled.

Chapter 4

The bottle flipped end over end, coming closer and closer to smacking Kristen right in the nose. Kia, still standing beside her, stuck out her left arm and snagged it out of the air. Kristen let out a sharp breath when the glass bottle smacked against Kia's palm. After bringing the beer bottle down from in front of her face, twisting the cap off, and taking a long swig, Kia glanced at Kristen and gave her a wink. She swallowed a few more gulps of the cold brew, took the bottle from her pouty lips, and turned to Kristen.

"Oh, I'm sorry, Kristen. Was this yours?"

That sent the other three girls into hysterics.

Kristen looked sheepishly from Kelly, Kara, Kristina then back to Kia and said, "Uh…nah. I better not. I mean, I'm only seventeen, ya know? Besides, I don't think my Mom would like me smelling like a brewery when I get home tomorrow."

"Duh, dumbass," Kelly chimed in, "it's not like you can't gargle with some Listerine and take a shower in Kia's bathroom before ya go home. Your snotty parents will never know the difference."

The other two girls sitting on the long black leather couch with Kelly just nodded their heads in agreement. Kristen looked back at Kia and said, "You think I should have one? I mean, I've never drank any sort of alcohol before, ya know?"

"Well…" Kia started to say but then brought her beer up to her lips and took another swig. "It's up to you, Kristen. We're not gonna force you to do anything you don't wanna do here tonight. We're not a bunch of savages, ya know. We're just a group of girls, that just so happens to have first names that all start with a 'K'… we call ourselves 'The K-Club' because—"

"*Anyway!*" Kara loudly interrupted. "We gonna watch the rest of this show or what, Kia?"

Kristen watched as Kia locked eyes with Kara. There seemed to be a non-audible dialog between the two girls told Kia couldn't say anymore why they called themselves 'The K-Club.' Kristen was nervous enough coming over, and now with the added peer pressure of having adding alcohol to the mix, she wasn't going to press Kia for an explanation as to why the girls hung out together *all* the time and called themselves what they did. Kristen decided to let it drop.

"Come on," Kia said, waving for Kristen to follow the rest of the way into the room to join the other girls.

"Yeah, okay."

As Kristen followed Kia to join the other girls on the couch to finish watching some sort of comedy show, she took a quick scan of the vast finished basement. Though, the term 'finished basement' wasn't quite right. To Kristen, it seemed more like a party center.

Turning her head slightly to the left and behind her, Kristen saw the side of the staircase that she and Kia had walked down, then a closed door (probably storage under the stairs), a pool table off in another room, a smaller room directly in front of her and through a doorway that looked filled with several arcade and pinball games, an air hockey table, a foosball table, and a dart board on the furthest wall. It looked like a hell of a fun room to play around in. Kristen wondered if after they were done watching the show if they would play some pool or an arcade game. She hoped they would.

As Kristen and Kia approached the three girls, Kristen looked past the carpeted center of the room with the leather couches and chairs and gigantic television (which rivaled the screens at Slippery Sliders, which made her wonder to Kia's parents had installed a pizza oven somewhere in the basement or the first floor of the house to bake their own homemade pies so they never had to go to the local town hangout and be among 'common folk'), to the wet-bar in the far corner of the room they were now entering. The bar was shaped like an 'L' and had a shiny wooden surface. The bar was accompanied by five tall-back leather barstools. The wall behind the bar was made of mirrors and glass shelves. Every square inch of each of the three shelves had a different bottle of liquor sitting on it. Almost all the bottles looked like they had been poured from at some point in time. There was a clock on the wall cattycorner to the mirrored part of the bar which said 'Burns' Bar'—after Kia's last name.

"I see you eyeing my Dad's liquor over there," Kia said, plopping into an oversized leather recliner and flipping up the leg rest. "Feel free to go over and pour yourself a shot of your poison if you're into that. Heck, if you're scared of smelling like a brewery tomorrow, even after brushing your teeth and taking a shower, liquor would probably be the way to go, especially if you stick to the clear ones. That's what Dad always says to his friends when they're down here drinking and watching the game on the boobtube."

Kristen thought for a moment and said, "Yeah, okay. Guess I can go for a...vodka...on the rocks...or something like that." Kristen had never had hard liquor before but did remember one time when her father had ordered one at a wedding they were at. It looked refreshing enough to Kristen, all clear like water with perfect square ice cubes floating on top. It seemed even more appealing when her father took his first sip from the rock glass and exhaled with an, "Ahhhh...hits the spot."

The four K's cheered their approval of Kristen's decision to have a drink with them. She walked past Kelly, Kara, and Kristina, sitting on the long black leather couch and up to the bar. She walked around to the back and stared up at the dozens of labeled bottles on the glass shelves. With all the bottles perfectly lined up with their labels facing out and the mirror behind them, it almost looked like a piece of art. Kristen heard Kia shout behind her, "If you turn around and look down, you'll find the glasses, ice maker, and stuff."

"Oh, okay. Thanks." Kristen replied, turning around and selecting a small glass from one of the four different kinds on a shelf under the bar. She placed the glass under the small icemaker and watched three perfectly square cubes of ice fall out and into her glass. She then turned around, grabbed a bottle of Absolut off the second shelf, twisted off the cap, and watched the clear liquor fall into her glass. She let the glass fill three-fourths of the way to the top and tilted the bottle back, stopping its flow.

Putting the bottle back where she found it, she picked up her vodka on the rocks and joined Kia, Kelly, Kara and Kristina, who had already pressed play on the DVR and were watching some fluffy guy talk in funny voices. Kristen said, "excuse me" and squeezed in between Kara and Kristina on the couch. Kia, still in the recliner with her feet propped up, looked over and winked. Kristen smiled and looked back at the big guy on the television.

As she watched some comedian named Gabriel Something-or-other, rant and rave and crack jokes about this and that, the four girls laughed almost to the point of falling out of their seats and rolling around on the floor clutching their stomachs. Kristen had trouble figuring out if she just didn't find the comedian funny or if her mind was still just too clouded from trying to figure out what she was doing in Kia's house with four of the most, if not *the* most, popular girls in the senior class. It really didn't make much sense, especially since Kristen was only seventeen (they were all eighteen) and a junior (with them all being seniors and graduating the upcoming spring).

Kristen noticed the hand she was holding the vodka on the rocks with was getting cold and passed the glass to her other hand. She still hadn't taken a drink of the clear alcohol. The truth of the matter was that Kristen had never taken a drink of any sort of alcohol in her entire life. Well, that wasn't all that true—when she had been a little girl, her father had given her a taste of his beer when her mother wasn't looking, but all dads did that with their kids at some point, and it hadn't been all that good anyway. In fact, if Kristen could still remember correctly, she had thought it tasted very bitter and had scrunched up her face from the taste. Of course, her father took the can of beer back and started laughing. Soon after, her mother had walked into the room and asked what was so funny. Her father didn't tell her, of course, in fear of more than likely getting yelled at for given their daughter a beer at the age of four, and had given Kristen a wink and a smile and stopped laughing after that. The thought of being daddy's girl even at such a young age brought a smile to Kristen's face.

Talking to her for the first time, Kristina turned to Kristen and said, "He's pretty funny, huh?" pointing to the fat comedian on the television.

Thinking fast, Kristen said, "Yup," and took a quick drink of vodka. It didn't taste bitter like the beer her father had given her but didn't taste all that great either. It burned on the way down her throat. Kristen swallowed hard, cracked a crooked smile across her face, and said, "Yeah. This guy is pretty funny...What did you say his name was, again?"

Kristen followed the four girls through the small door under the stairs and started descending another set of stairs. This flight was a lot narrower than the ones leading down to the basement and Kristen's shoulders kept scraping against the sides of the walls. She hoped that no six or eight legged bugs were being squished under the weight of her shoulders. She hated bugs with a passion and quickly thought of something else. Something a lot more pressing at the current time.

Soon after the comedian on the television ended, Kia had said, "Okay, girls. It's time."

Kelly, Kara and Kristina all got up from their seats and started following Kia out of the room.

Kristen sat there for a moment, not sure if she was included when Kia had said the plural form of the word, 'girl,' so she remained seated and took at sip of the melted ice in the bottom of her glass (she was also a tad light-headed at this point and was a little nervous to stand, in the event that she might fall flat on her face and be laughed at, therefore crushing her chance at being friends with The K-Club longer than past tonight).

Kia had noticed that she wasn't moving and had said, "Kristen. So? You coming or staying, sweetie?"

That's when Kristen knew *she* had been included in the girl's original plans, whatever they were. She stood and brought up the rear, following the girls out of the living room and through the small door under the basement steps, the same one she had noticed when coming downstairs behind Kia and just figured it was a storage space of some sort—broom, a vacuum, a mop, a bucket, sponges, dusting rags, and the like.

Now Kristen knew it wasn't a storage closet of any kind. Rather, it was a hidden staircase leading...Well, she still had no idea where. The darkness made it difficult not only to see if she was smashing bugs on the walls with her shoulders but to see the steps in front of her. She really hoped that with each step she took her foot would come down on a plank of wood and not have the sole of her sneaker catch the front edge of a stair and end up falling forward and crash into the back of Kristina, directly in front of her.

Once the girls were at the bottom of the stairs they took a hard left down a narrow hallway. If it hadn't been for holding onto Kristina's shoulder in front of her, Kristen knew she would have gotten lost in the total darkness. She was at least glad that even though the hallway they were walking down was narrow, it wasn't quite as bad as the staircase had been. Her shoulders were no longer rubbing up against the walls on either side of her, squishing creepy-crawlers along the way. Kristen felt Kristina stop in front of her. She took another step and quit walking. Judging from her now-bent arm, she was probably no more than six or seven inches away from the girl's back. Even though she didn't know Kristina, and the other girls for that matter, all that well yet, she was glad to be so close to someone. She could hear the other girls' breathing and the sound of her own heart pounding inside her small chest wanting to rip through her sternum and go scurrying off in search of light. That was about the time a small, vertical strip of light appeared about ten or so feet in front of her. She squint her eyes. The sliver of light grew wider and wider. Soon the entire hallway they had been walking down was aglow in flickering shades of yellow and orange. The girls started to move again and Kristen followed.

As they stepped through the doorway, Kia, Kelly, Kara, and Kristina fanned out around the room, Kristen moved to the last available place there was to stand. There were dozens of tall white candles burning throughout the twenty-by-twenty square foot room. On three of the walls were box-like shelves that went from the floor to the ceiling. In almost each box was a bottle of wine. Kristen couldn't tell what kind they were. She figured they were probably expensive given how the rest of the house looked. It didn't look like anyone had been down in the wine cellar for quite some time. The cork-topped bottles had a thick layer of grey dust and cobwebs all over them. Kristen wondered why someone would have such expensive bottles of wine and not at least dust them once in awhile. She assumed that Kia's father hadn't brought any of his buddies down into the cellar to check out his vintage stock in quite some time.

Looking away from the rows and rows and stacks and stacks of expensive wine bottles, Kristen turned back around and looked around her and saw that the four girls were evenly spaced apart. Their hands were clasped low, seemingly covering their crotches. Their heads were down, and their eyes were closed. Confused, but wanting to remain part of the group, Kristen folded her hands together in front of her and lowered her head…and saw what had been made out of masking tape on the floor.

A pentagram.

And she stood on one of its five points.

Chapter 5

"Hello?" Sherry whispered to whoever was on the other side of the door.

There was no response. Even the laughter she heard only a few moments ago was gone. It was silent. It reminded Sherry of how quiet the inside of a church can be if you visit during non-service hours. It was so quiet Sherry could almost hear her quick breaths echoing inside the bathroom.

"Hello. Is anyone out there?" she called out again, with a little more authority this time. "Anyone? Please? Someone answer me. Mom? Dad? Frankie? Frankie, this better not be another one of your jokes or I'm telling Mom and Dad." Sherry wanted to laugh after the last part if for nothing else then to make herself feel that everything was alright, even though she knew something was wrong.

Not hearing any reply, again, Sherry put her right ear up to the wooden door. She held her breath hoping to hear anything in the hallway on the opposite side of her bedroom door.

She heard nothing.

She let out the air she held in her lungs and took a deep breath.

Okay. Everything is fine, Sherry told herself. *It's just another one of Frankie's immature jokes that he always plays on me. Any minute now he'll knock on the other side of the door and send my bones jumping through my skin. I'll scream. And that's when he'll start laughing, again.*

But there were a few reasons why Sherry had a feeling that this wasn't one of Frankie's dumb, immature jokes that he always liked to play on her.

For one, she had just called out to her mother and father and neither of them had answered. *Because of what happened earlier?*

She silently reasoned. In the night when Sherry had gone to the door and opened it and had a bloody, naked girl fall on top of her, she doubted—even with her parents more than likely helping the girl right this minute—they would have come if *their* daughter needed them. Especially since she had knocked herself unconscious by banging the back of her head against the hardwood floor. Besides, it had to have been them who had taken her upstairs and laid her down in her bed to sleep off the dizziness that was almost non-existent at this point. So, yes, they must have been the ones to carry her upstairs, probably her father, to let her rest, which in turn had helped her recover from the frightening.

Secondly, because of what happened, Sherry felt more than confident that even if her parents were still busy taking care of the injured girl she had found on their front stoop they wouldn't let Frankie play one of his mean jokes on her, not at a time like this.

So, Sherry asked herself. *If it isn't one of Frankie's jokes, where the hell is everybody?*

That was the real question that Sherry had to find an answer for.

She stood up and called out, again.

"Mom? Dad? Frankie? Come on, guys. This isn't funny anymore. I'm okay. See? I'm up from bed and talking. There's no lasting physical damage here. Maybe a nice goose egg on the back of my head, but that's no big deal. So, come on, guys…let me outta here. The door is locked or stuck or something."

That's when the laughing started.

Again.

The maniacal laugh lasted for what seemed like several minutes, but was probably no more than fifteen seconds. *Besides, no one can laugh for that period of time without stopping to take a single breath, right?* Sherry didn't think so, but after the strange events from earlier in the night; her mother's ongoing strange behavior as of late and having a bloody, naked girl standing on their front stoop and conveniently falling on top of her when she opened the door, she couldn't be sure. Not anymore.

Sherry reached down and tried the doorknob again.

Locked.

Sherry didn't consider herself a fix-it-up type of girl, but she damn well knew the difference between when humidity made a wooden door swell, making it difficult to open and close, and when a bolt had been thrown to lock the door.

Definitely locked.

With a loud exhale, Sherry spun around on her heels and started walking to her desk in the far corner of the room. The dizziness in her head started to creep back and she wanted to sit down to think about the situation. At first she had thought about going back to the bed and lying down. But, that didn't quite seem like such a good idea. What if all of a sudden someone came charging into her room and she was half-in and half-out of sleep? The person would have the upper hand right from the beginning and by the time Sherry knew what was happening, the person would be straddling her hips and slicing her shirt off with a big butcher knife or something. Sherry didn't want that. Oh, no. So, instead of walking to the bed and resting, she opted for going to her desk and sitting in her chair. She was almost certain; unless she was close to death itself, that there wasn't even a remote chance she would accidently fall asleep in her desk chair.

She had argued with her parents for the last year or so about getting a nice, soft, leather one so she could be more comfortable when doing homework, but her parents had seen right through that plan. Her parents had told her that instead of pulling all-nighters for school, she instead would be staying up late on school nights and roaming the internet and therefore up to no good. Sure, her parents were hip (and had enough money) for her to have her own personal computer in her room, but the main reason her parents had bought it for her last Christmas was so she could do homework on it. Therefore, her parents' thinking behind her still having to sit on an uncomfortable wooden chair was that she shouldn't be tempted to doze off while doing homework. It was *work* after all, so what better way to be able to concentrate on the task at hand than to have to sit on something where she wouldn't get too comfortable. Her parents' reasoning didn't make much sense to Sherry, but who was she to say anything; even if she could (well, she could, but it more than likely wouldn't make much of a difference and she knew if she bitched about it too much, that they would just take away the computer and chair and she wouldn't even be able to surf the teen chat rooms late at night after her parents went to bed, so she mostly kept her mouth shut about the stupid, uncomfortable chair), anyway. Hell, when it came right down to it, she was the kid and her parents were the parents...or however the old saying went.

Sherry couldn't remember and didn't really care that much to.

She had more pressing matters to contend with.

Sherry sat down on the uncomfortable wooden chair and let out a deep sigh. The dizziness in her head was starting to come back and coupled with not knowing what the hell was going on just added to her fuzzy state of mind. Biting her bottom lip to keep from passing out, again, she leaned forward and reached under the lamp on her desk. Her father had never gotten around to installing the new ceiling fan with its 3-light fixture in her room, so all she had to illuminate the room the past month was the small Winnie the Pooh lamp she had had since she was five or six years old. Well, that wasn't the only reason she still had the lamp after so many years. The truth of the matter was she still liked it. It gave her a nice, warm feeling of times gone by when things were easier in her life—not having to deal with kids at school that didn't like her, the older boy at school that she liked but him not knowing that she even existed, homework, everything. Overall, she couldn't complain, though. She had a wonderful and loving mother and father (and brother—*ack*) and a few close friends who would do anything for her. And wasn't that what life was all about? The few select people you know who are always going to be there for you through thick and thin. Sherry thought so, anyway.

She grabbed the small, black twisty-thing underneath and lamp and gave it a turn to the right.

Click. Click.

Nothing.

What the...

She turned it again a few more times.

Click. Click. Click.

Still no light burst into the room to blind her.

The bulb must be dead, she thought, reaching under the desk, looking for her computer tower. After fumbling around for a few moments she found what she was looking for and pressed on the circular button.

Nothing.

She tried the computer's monitor.

Still nothing.

Damn it. Must a power failure or something. Either that or we blew a fuse. Yeah, that's probably it. Dad's probably stumbling around in the basement right now looking for the fuse box to flip a switch. Then Sherry remembered the bloody, naked girl. *Ohhh... Bet Mom and Frankie (bet he's loving it) are trying to take care of the girl and keep her calm till the paramedics get here, and now adding to that mess, we blow a fuse. Nice.*

But that didn't make sense, either.

In truth, Sherry had to admit, not much of anything was making sense to her just then. Her mind seemed to be floating all over the place, out of her control.

Focus, damn it.

After sitting in her chair for a little while longer, she finally got her mind back on track.

Okay... First things first.

Slowly standing up, Sherry shuffled to her bedroom window. Placing a hand on each side of its frame, she looked between the curtains and out into the night. God, how she hated that her family always had dinner so late. I mean, who in the world eats dinner at nine o'clock at night, anyway? Ugh. In truth, she understood it was because her father always had to work late and therefore didn't get home until quarter 'til nine and it had always been important to her parents (even with her mother acting how she was this past month—*I still wonder what is up with that? Maybe it's because she has to watch us kids from three in the afternoon till quarter till nine when Dad gets home and by that time we're about ready to drive her up the wall or something...*) that no matter what was going on in their individual lives, they were still a family and should at least be able to spend thirty to forty-five minutes together at the end of the day and share with one another how their days were. Yeah, when it came down to it, it did make sense to Sherry why her family was, like, the last family on the block to eat dinner so late, even on a Friday night when she could have been out with her friends, somewhere, anywhere. But, she did truly love her family (and, yes, even her snot-nosed, brother) and put up with it. Besides, she always had tomorrow—Saturday—to do what she wanted.

Squinting to adjust to the light coming from the street…

Wait just a dog-gone minute…There can't be any power failure…All the street lamps are on. And, hey…Across the street at old Ms. Wilkers' place…Her lights are on! So, yeah, a fuse must have just blown or something. Bet Dad will fix the problem in no time…

But, even with a fuzzy head and her thoughts bouncing all over the place, she didn't feel deep down in her gut that a simple blown fuse was what was going on.

She *knew* that something was wrong. It had to be. There was no way that her mother or father or even Frankie, wouldn't have come when she called out to them for help.

The door being locked was another thing that she hadn't thought too much about before.

There was definitely something wrong with the door being locked. Why? Because the only way to lock the door (with this being a close to a hundred-year-old house) was from the outside. And how would one lock the door from the outside? With a key. And where was the key? In the junk drawer in the kitchen. She knew her parents wouldn't have locked her in, especially not with the girl needing medical attention.

And…

Then, her mind did a full-circle back to the laughter outside her bedroom door.

The dizziness began to subside again—she had moved away from the window and back to the chair at her desk a few minutes ago—and, there was something else she could now recall about the laugh.

How strange it sounded.

How high-pitched.

And, then, right on-cue, came a thunderous knock at her bedroom door.

Sherry's bones nearly ripped out of her skin.

The knock was followed by the same, high-pitched laugh, she had heard before.

Sherry knew how her mother and father laughed and knew it wasn't theirs.

Not even close.

She also knew, sometimes unfortunately, how her brother laughed like when he was playing a joke on her.

Not even close.

It had to be someone else.

But, Sherry knew that when she had passed out from hitting her head on the floor after the bloody, naked...

Girl.

Yes, it had to be the girl.

Sherry's stomach dropped.

Chapter 6

"Dark Father hear our voices," Kia began, followed by the other girls, all except for Kristen who remained silent, staring down at what she was standing on. "We come to you in this hour to introduce you to our new friend, Kristen. She comes fully aware of her intentions to be part of our pact and to join you, our Dark Father, to rid the earth of those who are righteous and self serving. She welcomes up her soul, to burn in the glory of Satan for all of eternity and to do your bidding as you shall see fit. Amen."

Not knowing any of what the girls were going to say beforehand, Kristen said her own "Amen" and looked up from the floor.

The other girls were staring at her. They had a strange look in their eyes.

"Now you must strip," Kia said.

"Wh…what?" Kristen managed to stammer out.

"She said, strip, you ungrateful wench," Kelly snarled.

Kristen looked from Kelly to Kara to Kristina and back to Kia. She didn't know whether to laugh or shake in fright. She supposed the latter was in order for her particular predicament, but she also knew that if her bladder released now and she wet herself, her new *friends* would never let her hear the end of it. But, Kristen also knew it wouldn't just stop with the four girls in the room.

Oh, no.

They were the popular girls in school. The ones that had the richest parents, the nicest homes, the fanciest cars, the hottest, tightest bodies, the best looking boyfriends—everyone wanted to be with them—boys and girls, alike. But, if you couldn't be part of their group, the next best thing was to act like you were by making fun of whoever The K-Club chose as their next target to humiliate. Kristen already had enough problems going from public to private school. The teachers didn't instruct like they had at Oakwood

High, the kids weren't the same, and she rarely got to see any of her close friends anymore because she had to study ten-times as much as she had at Oakwood High. It wasn't because she was stupid by any means. No. She had been at the top of her class and it had been that very reason she had won the scholarship to come to Smithshire Academy to begin with. It was because of all the peer pressure to fit in socially and scholastically that made it hard for her to be her usual, studious self.

And now look at me, Kristen thought. *I'm standing here with a bunch of snobs that want me to make some pact with the Devil to do his evil bidding.* Kristen still didn't know what sort of 'things' she would have to do and she was afraid to find out.

Shit on me with a rubber turd.

Kristen finally took a deep breath, held it for a second, exhaled and said to Kia, "Are you shittin' me here?"

The four girls standing in the circle with her didn't laugh, didn't even smile. Though, they did eerily turn their heads simultaneously and look at their leader—Kia. The girl didn't even crack a smile. Her face remained stone-cold serious.

"We, The Killing Club, better known at school as, 'The K-Club,' shit you not, Kristen." Then she smiled. An almost scary grin that stretched from ear to ear—the other girls remained stone cold silent and focused on their leader.

"Uh…" was all Kristen could manage to get out of her mouth.

Then, Kia asked Kristen in a very matter-of-fact sort of way, "You want to be part of our group, don't you, sweetie?"

"Uh…yeah…I mean, sure. I guess so."

Kelly, the ever-cheerful-one spat, "You either do or you don't, girl. There are no ifs, ands or buts about this decision. You either are with us or against us."

Kara and Kristina both nodded in agreement.

Kara was the next to chime in. "You know, Kristen. Not very many girls in our school get this chance, you know. Especially not some snot-nosed junior. You're seventeen, for Christ sake. Can't you put these simple things together in your head, Kristen? Huh?"

Kristen didn't know what to say, so she just shook her head from side to side.

Next was Kristina's turn. "Kristen. You *are* the chosen one. Think about what Kara was just saying to you, 'you are only a junior and only seventeen.' Think about it—all four of us have been part of Smithshire Academy, are eighteen, and seniors. You were hand selected from all the other girls in the school with names that start with the letter 'K.' 'K'...for The Killing Club. Let me guess...you thought that 'The K-Club' was because all our names start with the letter 'K,' right?"

Kristen couldn't deny it. Yes, that is why she, along with everyone else in the school that she dared ask about it, thought was what the 'K' stood for...for The K-Club, The K-then-the-letters-that-make-up-the-rest-of-your-first-name, club. The Kia-Kelly-Kara-Kristina-Club. Yup, that's exactly what she thought the letter 'K' stood for.

"Yeah, I guess so," Kristen finally mumbled.

That's when the bond of silence was finally broken. All four girls started laughing at her. They were pointing their expensive, manicured fingernails at Kristen and laughing. They were laughing at how stupid she was, how ungrateful she was for being brought into the group and not showing respect to the four girls, and ultimately the Dark Father.

Kristen felt like falling to the floor, curling up into a tight ball and closing her eyes and never, ever opening them ever again. They could leave her down in the wine cellar for all she cared. They could leave her to age with Kia's father's expensive-ass wine. The bottles he probably loved just as much as the ones behind his expensive, perfect bar but didn't visit as often. Kristen wondered if Kia's father knew what was going on inside his wine cellar; the calls to Satan, the worshiping of the Dark Father, and all the other strange things that she thought probably went on down in the dark recesses of the house. Kristen could only guess Kia's father did know what went on down here and was too afraid to come down and do anything about it. Sure, he would be allowed in the recreation room in the finished part of the basement but that would be all he would be able to explore. Yeah, Kristen thought, that makes perfect sense why a father, as anal as he is with the rest of his house, would let his expensive bottles of wine get all caked with dust and cobwebs and the Lord above only knows what else.

"Kristen." It was the gentle, but thunderous sound, of Kia's voice shouting over the other girls' laughter. She said her name, again. "Kristen…Kristen…look at me."

Kristen slowly opened her tear, flooded eyes and looked across the pentagram to where Kia was standing.

Naked.

Kia smiled.

Kristen felt like she was going to vomit all over Kia's Dad's expensive bottles of wine.

She wondered if he would ever even know.

After fighting off the nausea, from not only seeing Kia standing before her naked, but the other three girls, Kristen swallowed hard and muttered, "Uh…I don't even know what to say, Kia. Really, I don't," and gave a half-hearted smile. At least she tried to.

Kia started to speak, again. "Like I said, now you must strip and show the Dark Father that you feel comfortable being around him. I mean, can't you feel him all around us right now? He's everywhere. He's in the walls, the floor, the wood racks that house my Dad's expensive bottles of wine…everywhere. He's in the four of us…and soon, if you let him, he will enter your soul as well and fill you with ever-lasting knowledge of how the world truly is."

Kristen felt confused and embarrassed. She sure as hell wanted to be friends with four of the most popular girls in school but didn't feel all that comfortable, at least not yet, being in her birthday suit in front of them. She decided to prolong Kia's talking as much as possible. She hoped it would work. At least for the time being—she'd just figure out how to keep Kia yapping until the time came for her mother to come pick her up tomorrow morning. She knew it wasn't going to be easy.

Kristen finally asked, "What do you mean when you said, 'he will fill me with ever-lasting knowledge of how the world truly is'?"

Kelly, the girl who Kristen probably liked the least, of course had to comment on her question. "What kind of question is that, girl? We are offering you ever-lasting knowledge from the world beyond from the Dark Father. Think about it, Kristen. He knows the evil ways of people., he sees them when they're sleeping and when they're awake…He knows all the bad things they do to one another. We have offered ourselves up to him because we are sick of how polluted the world has become with poor people, street bums that wander the street and stick needles in their arms filled with only God knows what…I could go on and on. The point is, we are here to do his bidding. We are here to rid the town, and eventually the entire Earth, of these horrific people and their miserable lives…"

The girl continued to yap away, but Kristen tuned her out. She really wanted to ask Kelly how she thought the four of them would be able to get rid of all the evil in the world but decided it was probably better just to keep her mouth shut and continue to listen to the crazy-talk coming from the naked girl. Kristen also didn't understand that if it were indeed true that they were in cahoots with the Devil, or the Dark Father, as they called it, why 'he' would be telling them to rid the world of all the people doing evil? It seemed to Kristen that if they were working with some evil force, that the being or whatever would want all the *good* people taken out and not the other way around. Regardless, Kristen decided it was best to just keep her mouth shut and listen to whatever the girls had to say. Maybe with some luck she would be able to show the girls the error of their ways and bring them back to 'good side.' She hoped, anyway.

Kristen finally realized what she had to do.

She would have to play along with whatever the girls were telling her to believe and do.

"Okay," Kristen said, "I think I understand what you're saying, now."

And she started to take off her clothes.

Thirty minutes later, Kristen found herself naked and covered in pig's blood while walking up the front sidewalk to a house with the lights still on. Obviously, the family hadn't gone to Slippery Sliders but instead had decided to spend a quiet evening at home together.

Kristen knew that the family's evening was going to be anything but quiet starting in just a few minutes.

Kristen looked behind her.

Kia's black BMW was almost out of site now, the further and further Kristen got to the family's front porch. The house's porch light wasn't on. Thank, God. Kristen thought about raising her hand up and waving to the four girls waiting inside Kia's car but thought better of it. For one, she didn't want to draw unnecessary attention to herself from some neighbor that might be looking out their window, and two, she honestly didn't want to do anything to upset her soon-to-be friends—Kia, Kelly, Kara and Kristina.

Besides, Kristen said to herself. *This might not be all that bad. I mean, really...All I have to do is walk up bloody and naked to a house, ring the doorbell, act like I've been attacked or whatever the fuck, and act like I'm passing out...*

It was what the girls told her she had to do after acting like she passed out is what was concerning Kristen.

Nah...They'll never make me go through with it to be part of The K-Club...

But then Kristen remembered what the girls told her what the name actually meant—it didn't mean that all the girls in their group had to have a name that started with the letter 'K.' Oh, no. What the 'K' in The K-Club actually stood for was—The *Killing* Club.

Oh my God!

They can't be serious, Kristen thought, still trying to convince herself. *Yeah, I'm sure they were just messing with me. I mean...I bet once I act like I'm passed out, the girls will come a-running and laughing their asses off, the people will be angry at first but then they'll understand that it's just a teenager thing and let us go (I hope), and we'll go back to Kia's house, I'll take a shower, and we'll hang out the rest of the night—maybe drink a little bit more, watch that fluffy comedian guy again or something. Yeah,* Kristen reasoned, *this is gonna be great.*

She hoped.

Kia's BMW disappeared behind a row of hedges that separated the house Kristen was walking up to and the neighbors. Kristen took a deep breath and continued forward. She could hear her wet feet quietly smacking the cement. The bare skin felt sticky and itchy under the weight of the pig's blood. Her once long, soft brown hair was now wet and stuck down to the top of her head, back of her neck and shoulders and was plastered against her cheeks. Kristen didn't even try to frown or smile, as she knew it would cause the stuck-on hair to peel the top layer of skin off her face. She continued forward.

As she neared the front porch and began to ascend the steps, an apple-sized pit formed in the bottom of her stomach. She choked down the rising bile in her throat as she stepped onto the innocent family's porch. She walked up to the door—and stopped. Her body shook all over from the embarrassment of being naked in public where anyone could and would soon see her, from being naked with something wet covering her skin, when it was only semi-warm out and from the fear of the unknown.

Kristen figured it was more than likely *fear* than anything else.

The fear was what bubbled deep inside her guts, telling her that when it came down to brass tacks, she really didn't have a choice. She wanted to be popular damn it. She was a smart girl—a very smart girl—and all she wanted was to be well liked by her peers. Sure, her getting good grades were all fine and dandy for her parents' sake, but what did it do for her? Nothing, that's what.

Fuck it.

She sucked in one final deep breath, reached up, and placed her finger on the doorbell, closed her eyes and moved her finger forward.

Ding Dong.

Chapter 7

Right when Sherry thought it couldn't get any worse, it did.

Now that Sherry knew that the girl who had fallen on top of her was in the hallway, Sherry started thinking all sorts of bad things. She imagined her parents getting robbed and tied to the dining room chairs, her brother being slapped for mouthing off to the crazed girl, and she would be next—locked inside her room with her parents already being held captive downstairs, Sherry could only wait. She took a deep breath trying to wash away all the bad thoughts floating around inside her head. It didn't work. She took one more deep breath before pushing herself off her shitty desk chair and walking back to the bedroom door. After the last knock, she hadn't heard anything else from the girl on the other side and hoped, really hoped to God, it meant she had vacated the house. Now the only thing Sherry needed to do was find some way out of her room and go help her parents.

As she walked toward the door an idea popped into her head and she spun around on her heals. She walked to the other side of the room to the bedroom window—the same one she had been looking out of only a short time ago. She had a plan—if you could call it that—to throw open the sash and jump to freedom. But, as Sherry got to the window she quickly realized the flaw in her plan: she was on the second floor of the house. Even if she were able to get the old window to budge, Sherry knew there was no way she could make it down to the ground without snapping a bone or blowing out her knee. It was a straight shot down to the ground, with no roof to step out on or even an overhang to grab onto and shimmy her way to someplace where she would be able to get a foothold and scurry onto a section of the roof. So, in short, doing any sort of Mission Impossible like jump from her window was out of the question.

She rested her still-throbbing head against the glass and peered outside. She could see tops of the tall trees that lined her street swaying in the breeze. She wondered if it were a warm or cool breeze and how it would feel against her sweaty skin. She longed for the night to turn into day and she would wake up all safe and sound in her bed and everything going on right now would actually turn out to be some sort of fucked up dream. She imagined what morning would be like: *she would throw her sheet off the top of her, grab her robe and wrap it around her and walk downstairs and into the kitchen. There, she would find her mother, father and brother sitting around the breakfast bar. Her mother and father would be chatting, drinking coffee, and reading the paper. Her brother, the little pain-in-the-ass, would be sitting at the bar and shoveling spoonfuls of Fruity Pebbles into his mouth. She would stroll into the kitchen, say, "Good morning, everyone," and walk to the refrigerator and pour herself a nice tall glass of cold orange juice. She would bring the glass up to her mouth and chug the entire thing then and there and not even take a breath while doing it. It would taste cold, bitter, and wonderful.*

The next thing that Sherry could imagine was her mother asking, *"What would you like for breakfast, dear?" (all nice and sweet like) and she would reply, "Oh, whatever you guys are having... You don't have to make anything special for me." Her mother and father would laugh. Frankie, would probably snort or make some other sort of crude sound. But then of course, her mother would tell her, "It's no problem, sweetie," and ask her in a very loving way, "Eggs over-medium, white toast, and bacon, right?" Sherry would nod, say, "Thanks, Mom," and pour herself another tall glass of orange juice before making her way over and sitting next to her brother. Heck, maybe she would even ruffle his hair right before she sat down and say, "Hey there, squirt. After breakfast how about we go out front and shoot some hoops?"* Sherry could imagine Frankie being so excited that multi-colored milk would shoot out his nose, and he could forego the rest of his 'nutritional breakfast' and race upstairs to get dressed and put his old sneakers on.

Yup, it would be such a fine, happy morning in the Laymon

household.

But, as Sherry rested her head against the glass and stared out into the night, she knew it wouldn't happen tomorrow or ever again. She wanted to break down and cry, let it all out, but she knew she had a job to do.

She had to figure some way to get out of her room without maiming or killing herself and save her parents from whomever the bloody, naked girl was or wanted from her family.

Yes. It was her family, damn it. Even if they had flaws, and Sherry realized that all families did have them, she loved her mother, father and yes, even her brother very much. She would be damned if anyone was going to mess with the people she loved.

With her heart pounding like mad inside her small chest, Sherry leaned back and was about to walk right to the door and give that bitch a piece of her mind…

She caught movement across the street in front of old Mr. and Mrs. Perry's house. Sherry knew the couple very well. Mrs. Perry had often watched her when she was a little girl when her parents had gone off to meet friends or have a date night or whatever. In fact, Mrs. Perry had even watched both her and Frankie together right before Sherry had gotten old enough to start babysitting her little brother by herself when her parents had to go away for a few hours. Sherry also remembered old Mr. Perry. Though not as gentle and kind as his wife, he had been a relatively nice man who mostly sat in his recliner, sipping on a brandy and smoking a big fat cigar, while watching his Detroit Tigers play on the television. Sherry knew from a very early age, if you were at the Perry residence and the Tigers were on the television, even if you were hungry or needed to pee or something, you always went to Mrs. Perry for assistance. It wasn't that the man was a mean old coot or anything—he just loved his Tigers and everyone else could just go run and jump into a creek when they were on the tube.

Sherry opened her eyes wide and stared across the street. Yup, there was definitely movement in front of the old couple's house. Though, with it being so dark outside and the busted street light never getting fixed (Sherry remembered her father calling about umpteen million times about it—the city telling him, that, 'Yes, we'll send someone out tomorrow,' and the next day would come, and no one would ever show up), there were so many shadows dancing across the Perry's front lawn that Sherry couldn't tell if it as Mr. or Mrs. walking around. Sherry wondered why, at whatever time of night it was right now (though, she thought it had to be well past nine because that's when her mother, brother and herself at first sat down at the dinner table with her father when he had finally walked into the door from another long day at work), why one of the elderly couple would be out wandering around. Sherry tried to think if they had a cat or something but couldn't quite remember either way.

Hhmm… Sherry said to herself. *Now that I think about it…I think I do remember Cindy, Mr. and Mrs. Perry's married daughter, bringing over a box of some sort about two weeks ago that looked an awful lot like a pet carrier. Yup. I bet that's it. Buddy or Goose or whatever the hell the cat's name was probably got loose somehow and made its way outside, and now Mr. or Mrs. Perry are scouring the yard looking for the poor thing.*

Poor thing? Sherry thought. Shit. If anybody is the poor thing around here, it's me and my family.

That's when two things happened: Sherry started pounding on the glass to get the old man's or woman's attention, and a split second later she heard the distinct sound of a skeleton key being inserted into the lock in her bedroom door.

Sherry twisted her head around just in time to see the door fly open and a red-black shadow come racing toward her.

She screamed but knew that if the old man or woman hadn't heard her pounding on the window to try and get their attention, the elderly neighbor across the street probably wouldn't hear her screams, either.

Chapter 8

Sucked into a foreign world, but strangely loving every minute of it, Kristen re-played in her mind what Kia and the other K-Club girls had told her on the car ride to the Laymon household.

"Okay," Kia had said, "the first thing you do when you get there is take a few deep breaths, walk up to the door, and ring the doorbell."

Kara and Kristina were giggling like school girls during Kia's instructions, while Kelly, the bitch, just sat next to her in the back-seat, brooding—about one thing or another. Kristen couldn't have cared less at the time what it was but had made a mental note to talk with her about it after her initiation was complete at the Laymon residence.

"Act like you were attacked or something," Kia continued. "No, no...Better yet, don't say a damn word. Act like you're half out of it or something. Then, whoever answers the door just act like you're passing out or some shit and fall right on top of them. Well, I guess falling on them depends on if it is a kid or a parent. I suppose that the parent would be quick thinking and big enough to probably catch you before you crash into them and flop against them as they land on the floor. Yeah. Anyway. Like I was saying... Just act like you pass out and fall into them. Hopefully, you'll get some young kid or something, and they'll go down like a sack of bricks. Then...ohhh...then...Just let them take care of you until you get a chance to take them by surprise and can start the ritual. But, remember, Kristen. Hey, Kristen...You listening?" Kia had finally asked her.

She had replied with a, "Huh. Yeah, sure...I'm listening."

"Okay, then. Anyway, you have to remember, Kristen...If you hear any mention of the word cops or EMS or whatever the fuck sort of grown up that could arrive on the scene and fuck up tonight's ritual…Your ass is grass at school on Monday, and you can kiss goodbye ever being part of the super cool K-Club. Got it?"

"Yeah, I think so," Kristen had replied.

Kelly then had reached over and slapped her hard across the face.

Kristen wanted to grab her burning cheek and ask her 'what the fuck is your problem, bitch?' but thought now, if ever, wasn't the time.

Kristen desperately wanted to be part of The K-Club. And even knowing how jacked up 'the ritual' had sounded in the wine cellar before they had loaded into the BMW and started to make their way to the Laymon house, she knew that come hell or high water she had to go through with it. Sure, she had had some doubts when she was listening to the girls in the cellar, and even more on the ride over listening to Kia's instructions on how to get inside the house, and even greater when she flopped on top of some young, cute looking girl who had answered the door…

But, now…oh, now…Kristen almost felt like she was born to do this. All of it. From slaughtering the three people she had already to what she was about to do to the sweet, young thing who had answered the door and started it all.

Yup, Kristen felt well on her way to be a full-fledged member of The Killing-Club.

Back in the living room of the Laymon household, Kristen smiled as she got back to work.

Her head felt like she had taken a dive off the high board down at the community pool, not having noticed before climbing the ladder that someone had drained the water, and smashed right into the concrete at the bottom of the empty pool. Her brain felt like scrambled eggs—and she had always liked them over-medium. She felt something warm and wet covering her from head to toe and wondered if she were lying on the bottom of the pool and bleeding to death, no one around to come and help save her life. Besides her entire head, her shoulders, arms, breasts, arms, pelvis, legs and even her feet hurt. If she didn't know any better, it felt like someone had taken a bat or something and smashed…

The girl!

Oh my God!

Sherry's eyes snapped open and jolted from side to side, looking around at the foreign environment she was in. No, she wasn't at the bottom of an empty pool and bleeding to death. Oh, no. It was much much worse.

Even with the dull pain in some places and red, hot shooting pain in others, Sherry still tried to move her head from side to side and her arms and legs. She couldn't do it. She felt like she was glued to the floor. All she could move were her eyes though her vision was limited being unable to move her head; moving her from one side to the other she was able to see she was lying on the floor in her living room (*thank God I'm at least still in my house*) and candles burned all around her. She caught a glimpse of something white (*chalk? paint?*) on the floor on each side of her body. There were so many weird things about her current state, Sherry didn't even know where to start—being on the living room floor, *glued* down there and not being able to move, the red, shiny stuff that appeared to be covering her face, the white thing on the floor, the candles—where the hell were her parents and brother?—all of it swirled inside Sherry's battered and dizzy skull.

"Ah, you're awake!"

The voice came from somewhere behind her, probably from a different room, Sherry figured—the kitchen? *Oh my God! There're knives and stuff in there*, Sherry thought and wanted to break down into tears. Sherry swallowed hard to stop the tears from bubbling up from her eyes and tried to remain calm.

Calm.

The thought of being skinned alive made bile rise into Sherry's mouth. She choked it back down and squeezed her eyes tightly— the pink sweat burning her eyes as it ran from her brow—she tried to scream but all that came out was a paltry whine.

The girl behind her started laughing again.

From the combination of the pain, panic, and fear Sherry now felt coursing through her entire body, Sherry began to hyperventilate and the lack of oxygen overcame the adrenaline. Sherry passed out again before the maniacal laughter stopped. As Sherry's eyes closed and she took in her last glimpse of light from the candles, she had no way of knowing the worst horrors of the night were only about to begin.

At least to her, that is.

By the time Sherry was passing out, her parents had already been slaughtered by Kristen who had used knives she had borrowed from the Laymon kitchen.

A combination of Sherry's father's, mother's, and brother's blood was what the almost-newest member of The K-Club had used to coat her naked body with.

If Sherry had been lucid, and could've raised her head to look past her feet, that's where she would have found the answers to her questions about her family.

They lay piled on top of one another—each deader than a doornail and drained of all their blood.

Chapter 9

Kristen looked down at the bloody, naked girl and giggled. The giggle soon turned into a deep laugh that shook her entire body. The fresh coat of rich, dark blood dripped and dropped on top of the girl each time she took in another deep breath of air to laugh again, each time harder than the last.

She reached down and slapped the girl across the face. Hard.

The girl screamed even before opening her eyes.

Yup. Just where Kristen wanted her.

The two girls' eyes made contact and stayed locked on one another. Sherry didn't know whether to scream, piss her pants, (she didn't know she wasn't wearing any pants or any clothes at all for that matter, yet) or do both at the same time. Sherry looked up in fear of what the stranger standing above her was going to do to next.

Another slap. This one across the other cheek. It hurt just as much if not more than the first. Sherry wondered how much more she was going to be able to take and also knew she didn't have much say in the matter and would just have to sustain whatever the girl wanted to do to her next. She hoped it wouldn't be worse than the fury of her hands but doubted that was going to be the case. The feeling in Sherry's gut told her it was going to get much, much worse very, very soon.

Kristen stood up, stepped over Sherry, and walked to the other side of the room. She came back with a bucket and a large knife. Sherry noticed that the sides of the bucket and the knife's blade dripped with red. She hoped, no, pleaded, that it hadn't come from anyone in her family. Though, the pit in her stomach told her otherwise. Not being able to take the macabre scene any longer, Sherry swallowed hard to keep down the still-rising bile in the back of her throat and spoke to the bloody, naked girl for the first time.

"Wh...wha..." Sherry was having a hard time forming words and getting them to come out of her dry mouth.

Kristen smiled and threw the knife at her head.

It thudded and stuck into the wood floor only inches from Sherry's right ear. Sherry tried to scream, again, hoping that she could get the attention of a neighbor or maybe someone passing by the house while walking their dog, but all that came out was a whisper of fear.

Feeling the power of The K-Club racing through her veins, like a bullet train to an unknown destination, Kristen walked to the girl and upended the bucket above her head. Sherry let out a quiet scream as she watched a red flood coming toward her face. A warm, coppery taste filled Sherry's mouth and washed over her eyes. Once she could tell the shower was finished, Sherry spat again and again trying to get the rancid taste out of her mouth and rapidly blinked her eyes to get the red haze from her field of vision.

Kristen laughed, again.

Sherry, finally getting some lubrication (though, not the kind she would have preferred), screamed.

Her scream was loud enough to wake the dead. Almost. Unfortunately, not even the ear-shattering, high decibel sound coming from an engine of a 747 was going to be enough to wake up her parents and brother, let alone a scream coming from a fifteen-year-old girl.

"Wh...what are you doing to me?" Sherry screamed, spitting blood up to the scary girl standing beside her. "Please...Just tell me what you want, and I'll get it or do it for you. I swear. Whatever you want from my parent's house or me or whatever the hell, just take it okay? Or, if you can't find what you've come here to take I'll help you find it. Just, please...Let me and my family go. Please." Sherry tried to keep tears from flooding her eyes. In some ways she wanted to cry, to wash away the rest of the blood from her eyes, but at the same time she didn't want to show the girl any more fear than she had already.

Kristen laughed. "I've only come here to take one thing... well...four things, actually...And unfortunately, sweetie, you can't really help me with any of them. Well, okay, I guess that's a lie. I've already taken three of the four things I've wanted…The fourth thing…well…I suppose if you really wanna help me you can, but I must warn you, it'll be worse that way."

Sherry had no idea what the fucking crazy girl was talking about so she said, "What the hell are you talking about? What do you mean you've already taken three of the things you came here for? What are you after; money, jewels, knickknacks…really… what the fuck do you want!?"

Kristen laughed and said, "Souls."

"Wh…what?" Sherry stammered.

"The souls of your family and you, my dear. I must collect four of them to appease the great, Dark Father, of the deep dark regions. This is my initiation to ever-lasting knowledge."

Sherry finally understood what the girl was saying. She came here for four souls and collected three already…

OH MY GOD!!!

My family…Mom, Dad, Frankie…NOOOOOO!

After the girl's screams finally died down, and she looked like she didn't have the energy to scream, much less talk anymore, Kristen stood with her feet on each side of the manic girl and started to recite the ritual prayer that Kia and the other members of The K-Club had told her. She held a burning candle in each hand, raised them to the ceiling of the living room and began speaking to the ever-knowing dark god.

"Dark Father…my name is Kristen, and I come to you with the fourth soul that you requested for my membership into The K-Club at Smithshire Academy, and when I descend into your brimstone world of fire and decay…let the souls of the three lying on the floor behind me and the soon-to-be released soul of this beautiful, naked girl quench your thirsty forked tongue and help us rejoice in the name of death and destruction that we mortals find all around us. Once partaking of this young flesh and soul, please let my four future sisters of The K-Club know I have fulfilled my duty as a wannabe and become a real member of the club and therefore be one of the most popular girls in school for the next year and a half to come. Amen." Kia and the other girls hadn't told her to say anything like 'be one of the most popular girls in school…' but

Kristen didn't think the Dark Father would mind all that much. In fact, she thought maybe he would find it a little funny or amusing and if anything, would like her for making light of a normally macabre situation that she was taking part in.

Kristen then reached to her right and picked up two buckets, one in each hand, filled to the top with the girl's parent's blood.

She then squatted down and sat on the girl's slick, blood covered stomach.

She let go of one of the buckets, reached out, and opened the girl's mouth.

Wide.

She then picked up one of the buckets and started to dump the blood inside her mouth. She didn't need two buckets of blood, and really only had to use a very small part of one of them, as she continued to slowly pour the blood into the girl's mouth until it bubbled over and started running down the sides of her face.

Satisfied the girl was no longer part of the living and her soul had passed to the Dark Father, Kristen reached over and grabbed hold of the butcher-knife that had been sticking in the floor on the side of the girl's head.

As Kristen held the blade close to the girl, she thought back and almost laughed about what she had said at the end of the prayer to the Dark Father. How she had thought '*making light of a normally macabre situation that she was taking part in.*'

And something in Kristen's mind snapped.

It was the part about 'taking part in…' that really got to her and she said to herself, t*aking part in, my ass. I'm fucking killing people here!*

Kristen hoped it was worth it, as she reached down with the butcher knife and slashed the young girl's throat.

Chapter 10

They could only see the outside of the second floor to the house. A tall wall of shrubs blocked the first floor, including the porch. It was the same wall that they watched Kristen disappear behind after she had gotten out of the car and started walking toward her target for the night. Now, two hours later, they continued to stare at the Great Green Wall and wonder what was happening on the opposite side and inside the house.

After they had pulled up to the curb two houses down from the Laymon house and Kristen had gotten out, Kia had killed the engine, twisting the key back so that radio stayed on to give themselves something to listen to while the pledge was still inside the house. The girls found that it was Movie-Theme-Song Night on 100.5 KROCK and they had spent most of their time trying to figure out what movie the song had been made for before the DJ told his audience at the end of each one. It had been a fun game, but after two straight hours of listening to the theme songs from *Rocky, Cocktail, Top Gun, The Goonies, Jerry Maguire* and the like, it was starting to get a little old.

Kia reached down and twisted the key forward. The opening theme song from the television show, *Friends*, had been playing at the time and was cut off in the middle of the band singing, "I'll be there for…"

"Hey!" Kia heard Kara shout from the backseat. "I was listening to that, you bitch."

Kia blew her off with, "Whatever," and turned back to staring at the shrub wall and the light that was still on at one of the top front windows. Kia wondered which family member's bedroom it was, if someone was still inside the room or if the occupant had just forgot to shut it off before going downstairs to find out what was going on with some strange, bloody naked girl standing on the family's front porch and ringing the doorbell.

"So, what do you think she's doing in there right now?" Kelly asked no one in particular.

Kristina, sitting in the front passenger's seat, twisted at the waist so she could see who Kelly was talking to. Then she said, "What did you say?"

"I said," Kelly replied, moving her head ever so slightly from side to side, "I wonder what that little bitch is doing in there right now...Besides, I didn't ask you, *Kristina*."

With that, Kristina turned back around and stared out the front windshield in the direction of the Laymon house.

"Anyway," Kelly continued, "what do *you* think, Kia?"

Kia thought for a moment and said, "To be honest, I have no idea. But I have a bad feeling that Kristen might have flipped on us."

"What do you mean?" Kara asked.

Kia turned to the girl in the backseat and said, "Well, think about it for a minute. How well do we really know Kristen, right? I mean, sure we've seen her around school and made fun of her and stuff, but before tonight none of us has ever even hung out with her. So, when you look at it that way, we really have no idea what she could be telling those people right now."

The three girls each somewhat agreed with a "shit" type of reply. Kia couldn't tell who said which one.

"Anyway," Kia continued, "I don't know about any of you, but I'm starting to get a little worried here, ya know. I mean, she should have been back a long time ago. Damn it! It doesn't take two flippin' hours just to walk up to a house and..."

"You don't think she..." Kara said, interrupting Kia's line of thought.

"That's the problem..." Kia replied, shaking her head back and forth and finishing with, "I just don't know. Hell, the last thing we flippin' need right now is the fuzz pulling up to the house and busting us all."

"Well then," Kelly countered, "why don't we just get the hell outta Dodge and let the police sort it out?"

Kia looked into the girls' eyes and replied, "You're shittin' me, right? Even if the girl did flip on us and the cops come, we can't just go taking off like bandits in the might. Shit. We're in a real pickle here. If we would take off and leave Kristen behind, the next thing you know the five-o will be knocking on my parent's door and telling them what we sent Kristen in the house to do. Hell, no…I don't know about the three of you, but that's just gonna fly with my parents. Sure, I can get away with a lot of shit, but if my parents found out we were up to this kind of sick shit, even if it is really only in our own little world and doesn't affect many others, they're still gonna crap a big, thick brick."

"We'll be lucky if all your and our parents do is 'crap a brick.' Shit. When you think about it, we could be put away from this type of shit," Kara said.

"That little bitch!" Kelly shouted from the backseat. "I'm gonna twist her little tit off if she rolls over on us."

Kristina, now hunched down in the passenger's seat muttered, "Do you really think she would tell the cops everything, Kia?" The girl looked like she was about to start shaking and break out into tears.

Kia reached over and gently placed her right hand on Kristina's left shoulder. She massaged it for a bit and replied, "I don't know, sweetie. I really don't. There's only one way for us to find out, though."

"What's that?" Kara asked from the backseat of the BMW.

"We gotta get outta the car and go to the house," Kia replied, in a very matter-of-fact sort of way.

The other three girls groaned but still knew she was right. They would have to get out of the car in the middle of the night, on a dark street, and start sneaking up to a house, making sure they weren't spotted by anyone on the way, and play Peeping Tom through one of the first floor windows. The girls didn't know if the windows to the house were covered on the inside with blinds or curtains, but they knew that something had to be done and soon. Sitting in the car and acting like a bunch of scaredy cats just wasn't gonna cut it. Not anymore, anyway.

"So," Kia said. "Are we in this together or what, girls?"

The girls didn't speak, only replying in various grumbles and groans. Kia hoped they meant, "Yes, we're in this together," but they sounded more like, "We're so fucked so why bother?"

They each took one last deep breath, tightened the belts around the trench coats covering their nakedness, opened the doors to the BMW, and stepped out into the dark, dead night.

The girls were only half way across the street when old Mr. Perry, who was still searching in the bushes around his house for the cat he and his wife had got not so long ago, saw their four half-bare asses trying to be sneaky while running low to the ground in a half-crouch across the street toward the Laymon residence.

Patrick Perry was and had been a great many things in his life; a die-hard Detroit Tigers fan, a great husband and loving father of two, an on-going community activist even in his old age...But most of all, he was a cop. A retired cop for the last fifteen years, but nonetheless, still a cop at the center of his being. He had fought and kicked the ever-living shit out of some of the most bad-assed motherfuckers around and had always had the eyes of an eagle. He not only still had 20/20 vision on his side even at the ripe old age of seventy-two, but his gut, his cop's gut, would turn into a pit the size of a grapefruit, when some bad guy would try to lie to him. Hell, Patrick 'Pimp Ass' Perry had always had the knack of being able to pick out the biggest dirt bag out of a bunch of everyday looking people. So, when he saw four teenage girls running half buck-naked across the street in front of his house, he knew what he had to do...

To call the good guys.

It's Miller Time, baby, Patrick Perry said to himself, leaping up his front porch steps and charging into the house like he was a twenty-one-year-old rookie cop on Monster Energy Drink.

Yup. It was time to call the police.

But first, before walking into the kitchen and grabbing the receiver off the hook to call them, he started up the steps to the second floor of his house.

To go to his bedroom.

To the nightstand beside his bed.

Where he still kept his freshly oiled .357 Magnum.

Chapter 11

By the time Patrick Perry had grabbed his big gun, thrown on a better pair of shoes, called the cops, and made his way out the front door, down the steps and into the street, the girls were gone. He jogged the rest of the way across the street, the big firearm held tightly in both hands as he moved toward the Laymon house. He finally slowed into a steady walk when he hit the sidewalk on the opposite side of the street. He looked from side to side. Nothing. From his current vantage point that was shrouded in darkness, he didn't see the girls. He knew it was time to start some investigative work—search the area, turn over every stone, and look behind every bush in the area until he found them. Patrick could imagine even now, without seeing where the girls had run off to, that once he found them the pit in his gut would be confirmed—they would be up to no good.

Patrick stepped off the sidewalk and onto the grass in the front yard of the Laymon house. He wasn't absolutely certain that this was where the girls were headed, but his gut told him he was more than likely correct.

First things first, Patrick said to himself. *I need to search the perimeter of the building, and I'll go up to the front door and ring the bell, make sure Stanley, Julie, Sherry, and Frankie are okay. If they are, which I'm sure they will be, I'll just inform them that some potential Peeping Toms are in the neighborhood, and it would be best to pull down the blinds so the girls wouldn't see them doing private family things.*

Yup. It sounded like a plan.

Patrick stopped for a second, listening to the slight breeze that blowing the leaves back and forth on top of the trees. He didn't hear any other sound; not a squeal of laughter from a group of teenage girls that was up to no good, heavy breathing, or the sound of their footsteps while trying to get away from him. Patrick held his breath for a second. Now he could hear the labored thumping of his heart inside his chest. At that moment, Patrick remembered what his doctor had told him only six months ago—that he needed to slow down and smell the roses, so to speak, to quit being so jumpy about things, enjoy the rest of his retirement with his wife, Martha, and let other people, the police officers that were still on active duty, worry about all the troublesome things that were going on in the world. But, the fact of the matter was, Patrick and his wife both knew that he would never be able to do such a thing. He had served in the line of duty for years and years and it just wasn't something you could give up—even if he had been retired for quite a while now. Being the watchful eye of the neighborhood had always been his personal duty, whether he was an active policeman or not. It was in his blood and deep within his soul. It was who he was.

Comfortable that the girls weren't within ear or eye shot distance of him, Patrick blew out the breath he had been holding and started walking again. He strode past the tall wall of hedges that separated the Laymon from the Ketchum household and started walking on the side of the house toward the backyard. In his mind he thought back to the good ol' days when he was an active duty police officer and how many times he and his partner had had to do a sweep of a yard while looking for a bad guy. Back to front yard was the way he had always done it, so that was exactly what he was going to do this time.

Even though Patrick couldn't hear or see the girls anywhere, he still had a feeling something wasn't quite right. Maybe it was the smell in the air, maybe just that seeing a gang of half bare-assed teenage girls running loose on the streets at eleven-thirty at night made a pit form in the bottom of his stomach that told him that they were up to no good.

He didn't know, yet.

But he was damn sure going to find out.

As he entered the backyard, Patrick raised the hand-held cannon to chest level and readied himself for whatever lie ahead.

Laying on the ground in between shrubs, Kia, Kelly, Kara, and

Kristina, watched the old man pass no more than fifteen feet in front of them and walk toward the back of the house. They followed him until all they could make out was a gray shadow of his existence. Then he was gone. Disappearing into the pitch black backyard.

Kelly turned toward Kia, no more than two feet from her, and whispered, "Who the hell was that?"

"Hell if I know," Kia whispered back. "But did you see what he was carrying?"

"Yeah...I saw it too." That was Kristina.

Kelly and Kara both said at the same time, "What? What did he have?" Kara added, "I swear to God, Kia...if you say he pulled out his wrinkled penis or something, I'm gonna puke my guts out."

"I think I saw him pull out a gun," Kia replied in a very matter-of-fact sort of way.

Kelly and Kara both let out a gasp. Kelly said, "Shit."

"So, what are we gonna do, now?" Kara asked after a few seconds had passed.

"Well..." Kia began. She could tell she had all the girl's attention with the revelation that a potentially crazy old guy walking around with a loaded gun had been brought to their attention. She looked from side to side and saw that all the girls' eyes were intently focused on her. Even in the dim light from the moon above, she could tell by frowns on the girls' faces that they were worried. Hell. Truth be told, Kia had to admit she was just as scared as any of them were right now. Before she continued, Kia even thought about telling the girls "the hell with this...let's just get back in the car and get the hell out of here" but knew she couldn't do that. She knew if it came right down to it, they could handle some guy with a gun that was probably too old now days to even hold the firearm steady. So, no. She wasn't worried about the old guy. What she was worried about was if the old guy had called the cops before coming out of nowhere and starting to investigate on his own. *Maybe he is a cop,* Kia said to herself, then quickly dismissed the idea. *Nah. He's too fucking old to be one. He probably heads up the local Community Watch and thinks of himself as a badass or something. Yeah, that's probably it. Probably not even a real gun at all. Well, it's probably real but not real real. The thing probably shoots bee-bees or pellets instead of ammunition. Yeah, that has to be it.* She hoped. Finally, Kia looked one last time to the girls on each side of her, then continued in a whisper, "I think we should still try to get in the house or at least peek in a window and see what is going on. I really don't know what that old fucker is up to, but his bark is probably worse than his bite. Besides, I doubt the thing was even a real gun, ya know. At least not one that shoots bullets, anyway. It's probably a bee-bee gun he bought at Wal-Mart so he could sit on his front porch in the mornings and shoot a squirrel or two while drinking his coffee."

"Uhhh…Why the hell would he shoot squirrels?" Kara asked.

"Hell if I know," Kia replied. "Maybe the rat bastards were getting in and eating all the seed out of his bird feeders or something. I don't know. You know how old people like to feed the birds down at the park, right? It's probably the same over in his yard. He sits on the front porch in the mornings, sipping his coffee, and holding his bee-bee gun, just waiting for one of those overgrown gray rats to run up a tree and climb down to nab a little snack out of one of his bird feeders."

"Oh. Okay." Kara.

"Sounds believable." That was Kristina.

"You're full of more shit than a goose. That old guy doesn't have any gun. It's probably his bottle of Maalox or something. The old bastard is probably so scared of being outside at night that he's about ready to shit his pants at the littlest sound. Hell. I think we should bum-rush him and see if his shooter quirts." And that was Kelly. Of course. Always willing to shit on your Sunny Sunday Parade.

Ugh.

Kia took one final look in the direction where the old man had disappeared and was about to motion for the girls to "come on, let's go" when a plan of action came to her.

It was a very simple one at that.

To go up to the door and ring the bell. Then whomever answered, just explain that their car broke down, they saw a light on inside the house, and figured that someone was still awake, and hopefully they would be kind enough to let them come inside really quick and use to phone to call AAA or maybe one of their parents to come and pick them up. That's when they could see what the fuck Kristen was doing and if she was ratting them out and having one of the family members call the cops.

It sounded like a swell plan.

There was one problem, of course. What if the man or wife or hell, maybe even one of the kids, questioned that they all wore the same thing—a trench coat with nothing underneath. Of course, they wouldn't be able to actually *see* that they didn't have anything underneath their coats but would more than likely be able to assume as much. In fact, it wouldn't be all that hard at all to figure out the girls were naked underneath the coats because their legs were bare and a little too much skin showed in the 'V' of the coat's collar. Then they might put two and two together—that all *five* girls were up to no good—and they would call the cops. Besides, what five self-respecting girls would go driving around town or even coming back from Slippery Sliders at eleven o'clock at night without wearing much of anything?

Even so, she hoped it would work.

Because when it came right down to it, they didn't have any other option.

They had to find out what Kristen was doing.

Not for her sake.

Oh, hell no.

But for their own.

For the well-being of the true members of The K-Club.

Kia said, "All right. Enough of this lying around like a bunch of pussies. Let's go find out what *our* girl is doing in there."

But, right before they were going to scurry out from underneath the shrubs they had been hiding under, a dark moving shadow appeared from the far front side of the house. Soon it was in enough moonlight to see who it was.

The old man.

Again.

Sonofabitch, Kia said to herself, motioning for the girls to stay put.

They watched the old man, who was definitely holding a gun in front of him, climb the front porch steps and press the doorbell.

Chapter 12

Kristen heard a sound coming from the front porch even before the distinct *ding dong* of the doorbell resounded through the house. It sounded like shoes scraping against wood.

Just what the dead and soon-to-be dying victims ordered.

Well, sort of.

She was sure they would have still chosen to be alive right now, instead of three of them, a man, woman, and a small boy, all sliced and diced and drained of their blood and piled like a stack of French fries in the middle of a greasy plate. But it wasn't a greasy plate coming from the kitchen at Mel's Diner. Oh, no. It was the family's living room. The same place where the family had more than likely spent countless hours enjoying each other's company by playing board games, watching television, talking about their work and school days, the whole nine yards. If Kristen didn't want with all her ever-living heart to be part of the coolest girls' club in school, she would almost feel sorry for them. Actually, she knew she would feel more than sorry for what she had done to them—she would feel mortified and ashamed. But, the fact of the matter was, she *did* want to be part of The Killing Club, err, The K-Club, and if it took a few slain bodies of people she didn't even know to become a full-fledged member, she would do what she needed to do. Hell, what she more than three-fourths had done already.

Kristen half-smiled, half-frowned, as she hid the large butcher knife, the one she had been working the girl with, behind her back and stood up and started walking across the living room toward the front door.

She hoped it wasn't the cops.

That would be bad news.

Really bad news.

Not only had she yet to release the girl's soul, making her goal of four released souls to become an official member of The Killing Club, but she would be arrested, as well. That would cause a shit storm all on its own. Not only would she not be able to be part of the most popular girls' club at Smithshire Academy, she would be hauled off to jail, be put on trial, and be convicted of three first degree murders and one attempted murder. Then, she would have to watch her parents, crying their eyes out, as she was dragged out of the courtroom in shackles and chains to meet her destiny on death row.

Ding Dong.

Kristen, still buck-naked and bloody from head to toe was in no way, shape, or form suitable enough to be opening the front door and have someone that she didn't even know (*not that I'd be all that comfortable with a man I did know seeing me naked...*), be staring back at her.

Ding Dong.

Goddamn!

Kristen came up to the door and put her eye up to the peephole.

She thought about flicking on the front porch light so she could see better, but as she stared out the tiny glass hole, she could tell there was really no need.

Because she could see just fine.

It wasn't the cops at all.

Just some old man who looked like he was lost and needed directions to find his way back home.

An old man.

A *fifth* soul.

Kristen smiled.

It was like a bonus from the Dark Father.

She smiled again, as she grabbed the doorknob, twisted and pulled the door toward her, as she brought the hand that was holding the knife from behind her back.

The smile turned upside down as she came face to face with the old man.

An old man holding one big fucking gun.

Kristen slashed out with the knife.

It was followed by the bark of the big bad gun.

Chapter 13

The original members of The K-Club watched from the bushes as Kristen tried to slice the old man and a split second later saw her body buck from the loud explosion coming from the old man's gun. The girls heard Kristen drop to the floor with a loud thud. The old man then lowered his gun, stepped over a bleeding Kristen, and entered the house. He seemed to disappear inside forever, but it was probably no more than thirty seconds, until he came charging out of the house, gun held up into the air, jumped off the porch with one flying leap, and come crashing down in the grass by the sidewalk that led to the front porch steps. He coughed and hacked away until a flood of liquid came shooting out of his mouth and went splashing onto the nicely manicured front lawn. As they watched the old man puke his guts out, each of them silently wondered what went on inside the house.

Finally, Kara broke the silence that was enveloping the four girls. "What the fuck do you think he saw in there?" she asked, trying to keep her voice as low as possible. Sure, the old man was still hacking his dinner out onto the grass, but he still had the gun and it scared the piss out of each of them. They definitely didn't want to get caught up in a one-way firefight.

"Who knows," Kia whispered in reply.

"Whatever it was," Kristina said, "it couldn't have been good."

"No shit, Sherlock…Where's the squad car?" Kelly, of course.

"Okay," Kia began. "The last thing we need to do is start jumping to conclusions, ya know. I mean, we don't know what he saw in there, and each of us is more than likely laying here in the damp grass thinking the worse."

"Yeah," Kara agreed. "Maybe he just had a bad reaction from shooting Kristen in cold blood, ya know."

"He didn't shoot her in 'cold blood,' dumbass. Hell. Did you

see what she tried to do to him after she answered the door? Shit…
If I were some guy and some chick tried to cut off my junk, I'd
probably shoot a bitch too," Kelly said and snickered to herself.

A look of fear and disgust formed on the faces of Kara and
Kristina.

Kia turned to Kelly, shook her head and said, "We really don't
need your smart-assed mouth right now, Kelly. If you can't act like
someone that could get busted and go to jail, i.e., the four of us,
then you might as well just take your chances now and haul ass out
of here and risk either getting blown away by Mr. Old Man Puke
over there or…"

"Whoa whoa whoa," Kara interrupted. "What do you mean,
'someone that could get busted and go to jail'? Like who? Us?"

"Of course she means 'us,'" Kristina whispered a little too
loud.

"Hey, Kia," Kara said. "What do you mean?"

Kia didn't have the energy to reply anymore. She continued
to watch the old man, who was still carrying his cannon of a hand
gun, as she stood up, wiped the puke off his mouth with the back
of his left hand, and listened as the distant sound of sirens started
up. She knew where they were coming.

To the very same house that they had sent Kristen into to do
'the Dark Father's bidding.'

Oh dear Lord…What have we done?

The sounds of a future prison sentence and possibly the electric
chair started to descend upon them.

Chapter 14

By the time the shitload of police cruisers, fire trucks, ambulances, and a large gathering of on looking neighbors behind the yellow *Caution* tape was on the scene, it had been hectic enough for the girls to slide out from under the wall of bushes they had been hiding under. At first they thought about leaving, fleeing for their lives, getting as far away as possible just in case anyone might suspect (especially the gun carrying old man) they were involved in whatever had happened inside the house. But, the truth of the matter was, they had to find out. So, instead of retreating to the relatively safe confines of Kia's BMW and zooming away from the crime scene, they quietly joined the flood of other people trying to figure out just what the hell had happened inside their neighbor's home.

The girls heard a variety of second-hand accounts of what happened inside the house, including, "They say it was a blood bath in there," "I heard that Stanley finally found out about his wife's affair with the tennis pro and just snapped and slaughtered the whole damn family," and "It's a shame that something like this has to happen in our quiet neighborhood…What's the world coming to?" and the like. Each voice of opinion sent chills down the spines of the girls, who realized that at least in some small way they were responsible for what happened—whatever it was—they still had no idea. But, from the sheer quantity of law enforcement and paramedics on the scene, they guessed it wasn't going to be good.

That's when the first of the body bags started to be carried from the house and slid into the back of a waiting ambulance. Once the bag had been placed inside, the lights on top of the truck went out, and it slowly started to pull away from the scene.

Body bag after body bag was carried from the house.

The girls had counted three so far.

That meant that there were still two of them—dead or alive—in the house. Kia and the rest of The K-Club hoped one of the survivors was Kristen. Then again, maybe it would be better if their little secret of "worshipping the Dark Father" had died right along with her.

Kia was lost in thoughts when a rather rotund woman that was standing behind them wearing only a muumuu shouted, "Look! Someone. Look, everybody!"

A mixture of cheers and moans spread through the crowd.

Cheers for someone still being alive.

Moans for what she looked like.

Everyone pushed forward for a closer look at the macabre remains of the survivor.

A girl who looked to be about fifteen or sixteen, with flowing long brown hair and a smooth and tight bloody naked body, was rolled out of the house and hurried to the open back of a waiting ambulance. A moment later its sirens started wailing through the cool Fall air. It screeched away from the scene a moment later.

That makes four…three dead, one alive, Kia said to herself.

All of them wondered in hushed tones if the last person carried from the house would still be alive or zipped up nice and tight inside the dark confines of a black body bag.

A hush fell over the crowd.

And a gurney carrying a still-alive Kristen was rolled from the house by three paramedics. The old man with the gun walked lazily behind the rest of the authorities. Kristen was still bloody and naked. One of the medics, a cute, young guy was holding a thick pad of gauze over her right breast where the non-fatal bullet had punched through her skin.

A wave of both dread and joy rushed through each of the girls as they pushed their way to the far side of the crowd beside the last ambulance left on the scene.

Luckily, they were able to make it to the front of the line.

The girls of The K-Club watched as two of the medics continued to work on Kristen, while the third hurried ahead to open the back doors of the ambulance.

They rolled the badly injured Kristen up to the back of the

truck and stopped.

The three medics then took their positions to hoist the gurney into the back of the ready-to-go life-saving mobile.

One of them said, "Okay. On the count of three, fellas."

The K-Club girls looked down at the badly injured and barely still-alive Kristen.

"One."

Kristen coughed up some blood. It ran off the side of her face and onto her neck. One of the medics turned her head to one side so she wouldn't choke to death on her own blood.

The same side where The K-Club girls were standing no more than five feet away.

"Two."

Kristen's face scrunched up into the most painful look Kia had ever seen on another person.

In that instant, Kia had a moment of truth about herself, about what *they* had done to some poor, innocent girl from the wrong side of Millionaire's Row. It wasn't right. Hell, they had sent a girl in to do some dastardly deeds and hadn't even meant for it to happen the way it did. The fact of the matter was, none of the girls in The K-Club thought that another person would ever stoop to such low levels just to be part of the most popular girls' club at Smithshire Academy.

"Three." The paramedics started to hoist Kristen into the back of the waiting ambulance.

That was the point when it dawned on Kia that she wouldn't be able to live with herself if *they* continued to lie to the poor, innocent girl any longer. So, she mouthed, "I'm sorry."

Kia saw Kristen's eyes go wide and instantly fill with tears of total betrayal.

Kristen had trusted 'The K-Club,' and the girls had let her down.

Kia nodded to the girls that it was time to go.

They turned and started walking away from the girl they betrayed because they thought it would be a funny thing to do—to make up being 'The Killing Club,' practicing the Occult, wanting Kristen to be part of the popular kids in school—all of it.

As they crossed the street, walking toward the BMW, Kia thought she heard Kristen call out to them, "Wait…" but figured it was just the cool Fall breeze blowing through the remaining leaves on the trees and that it was only playing tricks on her ears.

Chapter 15

"Hey! You there!" came a raspy voice from somewhere behind them.

All four girls twisted around at once and saw a dark shadow walking toward them.

As the shadow came out of the dark patch of street in front of the house where all the horrible acts were committed and into the patch of road where a street light still burned bright, the girls recognized who it was.

The old man with the gun.

He held it in front of them, pointing it in their direction.

Yes.

As he strode toward them, Patrick recited in his head what the near-dying girl in the back of the ambulance had told him—that she had been tricked and that the group of girls that were just standing by the ambulance were the ones that told her to do it.

He had tracked them down just like the good ol' days.

Patrick Perry ordered the girls to get down on the ground and put their arms out in front of them.

Another bad guy, err, girls, bite the dust, he said to himself.

Patrick smiled, as the pounding of his brothers' footsteps came thundering up the street behind him.

He was still on the job and always would be.

About the Author:

Ty Schwamberger is an award-winning author & editor in the horror genre. He is the author of a novel, multiple novellas, collections and editor on several anthologies. In addition, he's had many short stories published online and in print. Three stories, "Cake Batter" (released in 2010), "House Call" (released in June 2013) and *"The Halloween Hero"* (optioned in 2014), have been optioned for film adaptation. He is an Active Member of the International Thriller Writers. Learn more at http://tyschwamberger or follow along at @SchwambergerTy.